STONE ARCH BOOKS
a capstone imprint

STONE ARCH BOOKS™
Published in 2014
A Capstone Imprint
1710 Roe Crest Drive
North Mankato, MN 56003
www.capstonepub.com

DC Comics
1700 Broadway, New York, NY 10019
A Warner Bros. Entertainment Company

Cataloging-in-Publication Data is available at the Library of Congress website:
ISBN: 978-1-4342-9214-8 (library binding)

Summary: Thunder and Lightning strike in the middle of Jump City! But when Cyborg and Beast Boy get involved, it turns into a massive free-for-all battle royale. And you know what that means: lots of property damage! Follow Robin, Beast Boy, Cyborg, Raven, and Starfire as these teenage super heroes team up to take down super-villains and schoolwork alike.

STONE ARCH BOOKS
Ashley C. Andersen Zantop *Publisher*
Michael Dahl *Editorial Director*
Sean Tulien *Editor*
Heather Kindseth *Creative Director*
Alison Thiele *Designer*
Tori Abraham *Production Specialist*

DC COMICS
Lysa Hawkins & Tom Palmer Jr. Original U.S. Editors

Printed in China.
032014 008085LEOF14

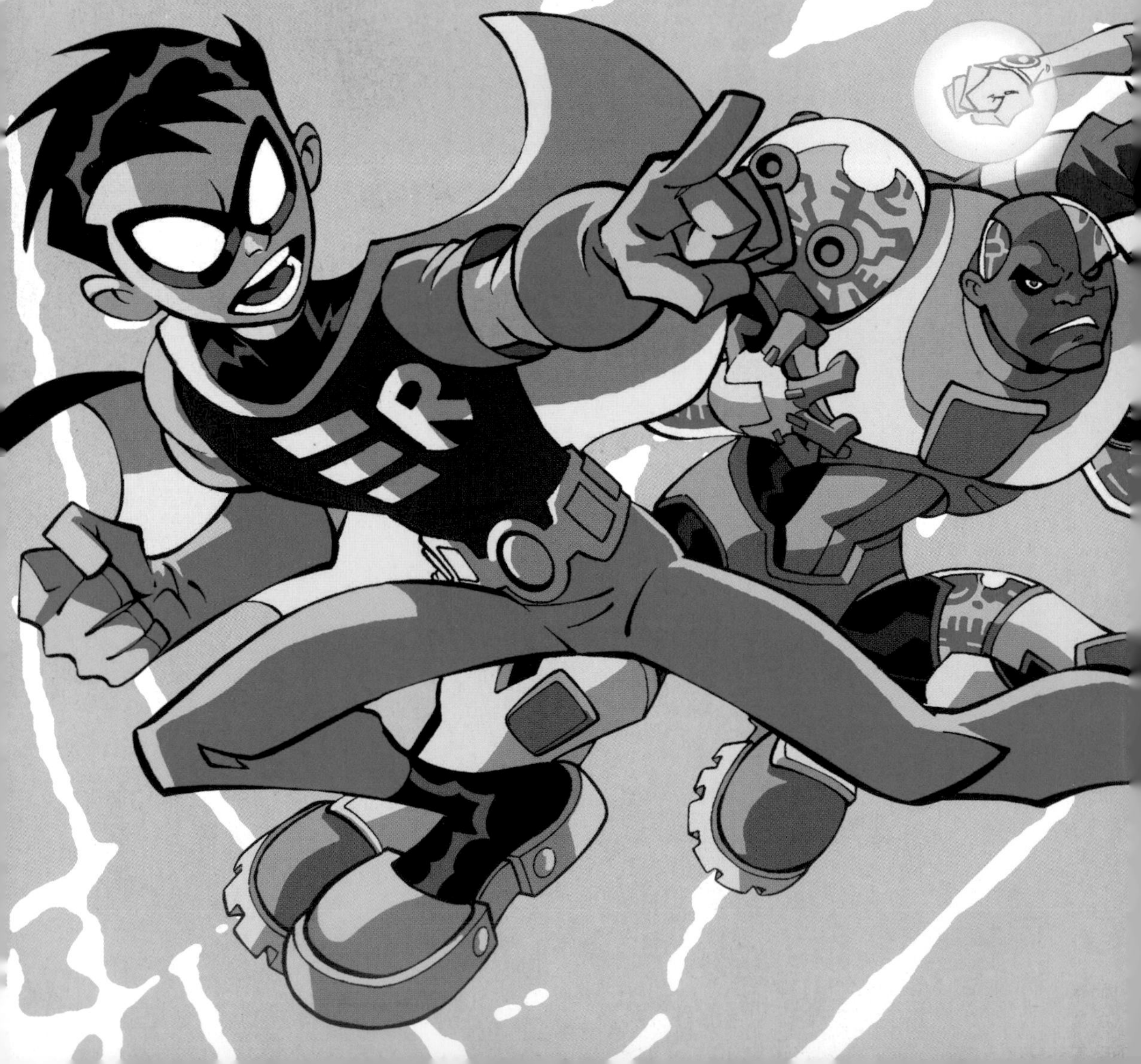

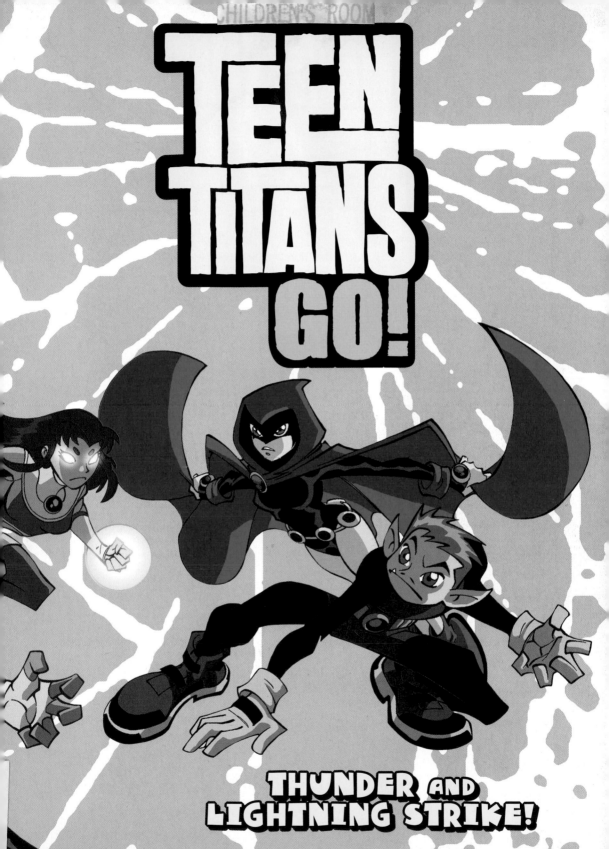

TEEN TITANS GO!

THUNDER AND LIGHTNING STRIKE!

J. Torres .... writer
Todd Nauck & Larry Stucker .... artists
Heroic Age .... colorist
Phil Balsman .... letterer

TEEN TITANS GO!

ROBIN

REAL NAME: Dick Grayson

BIO: The perfectionist leader of the group has one main complaint about his teammates: the other Titans just won't do what he says. As the partner of Batman, Robin is a talented acrobat, martial artist, and hacker.

STARFIRE

REAL NAME: Princess Koriand'r

BIO: Formerly a warrior Princess of the now-destroyed planet Tamaran, Starfire found a new home on Earth, and a new family in the Teen Titans.

CYBORG

REAL NAME: Victor Stone

BIO: Cyborg is a laid-back half teen, half robot who's more interested in eating pizza and playing video games than fighting crime.

RAVEN

REAL NAME: Raven

BIO: Raven is an Azarathian empath who can teleport and control her "soul-self," which can fight physically as well as act as Raven's eyes and ears away from her body.

BEAST BOY

REAL NAME: Garfield Logan

BIO: Beast Boy is Cyborg's best bud. He's a slightly dim but lovable loafer who can transform into all sorts of animals [when he's not too busy eating burritos and watching TV]. He's also a vegetarian.

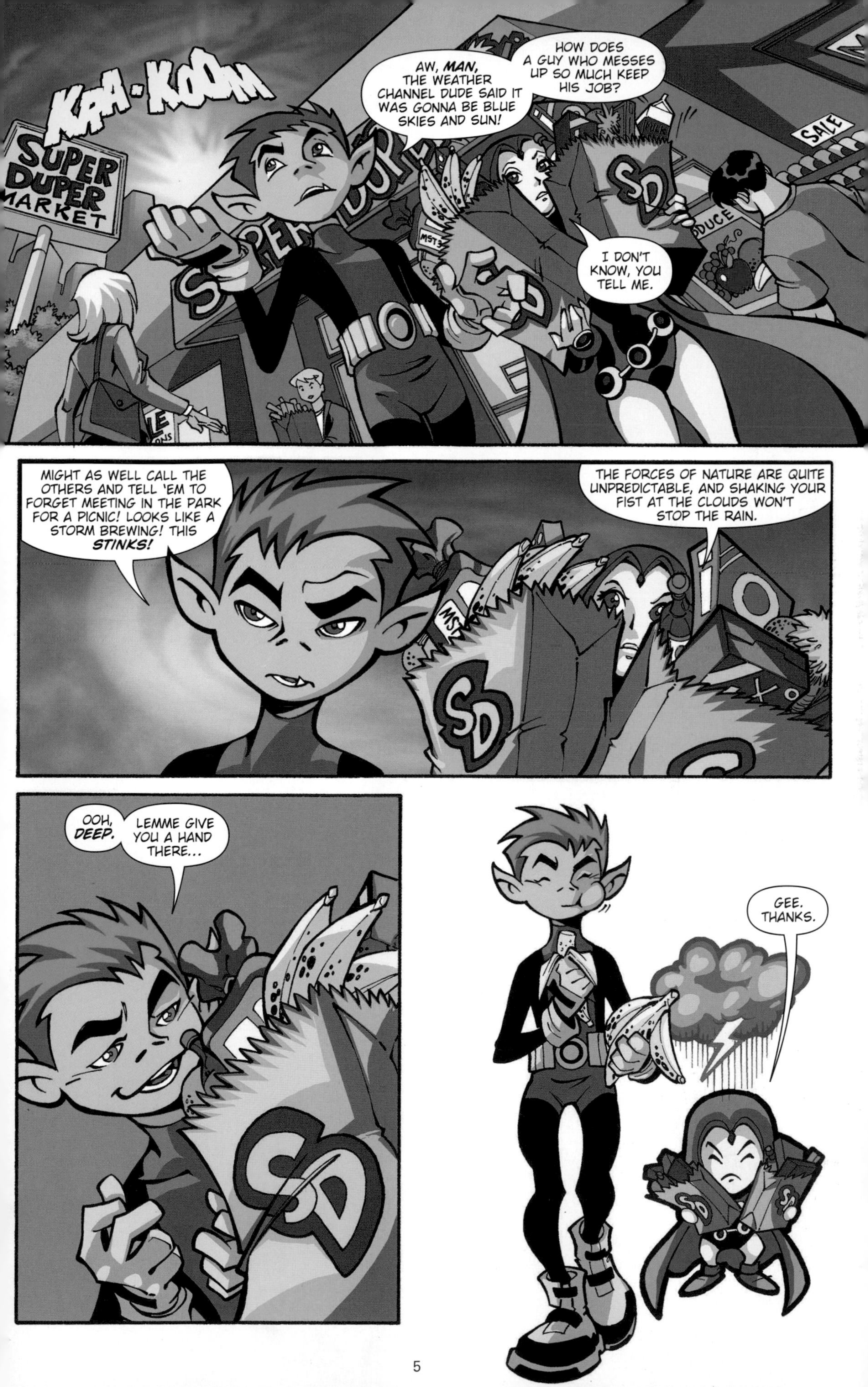
KRA-KOOM
SUPER DUPER MARKET
AW, MAN, THE WEATHER CHANNEL DUDE SAID IT WAS GONNA BE BLUE SKIES AND SUN!
HOW DOES A GUY WHO MESSES UP SO MUCH KEEP HIS JOB?
SALE
I DON'T KNOW, YOU TELL ME.
MIGHT AS WELL CALL THE OTHERS AND TELL 'EM TO FORGET MEETING IN THE PARK FOR A PICNIC! LOOKS LIKE A STORM BREWING! THIS STINKS!
THE FORCES OF NATURE ARE QUITE UNPREDICTABLE, AND SHAKING YOUR FIST AT THE CLOUDS WON'T STOP THE RAIN.
OOH, DEEP.
LEMME GIVE YOU A HAND THERE...
GEE. THANKS.

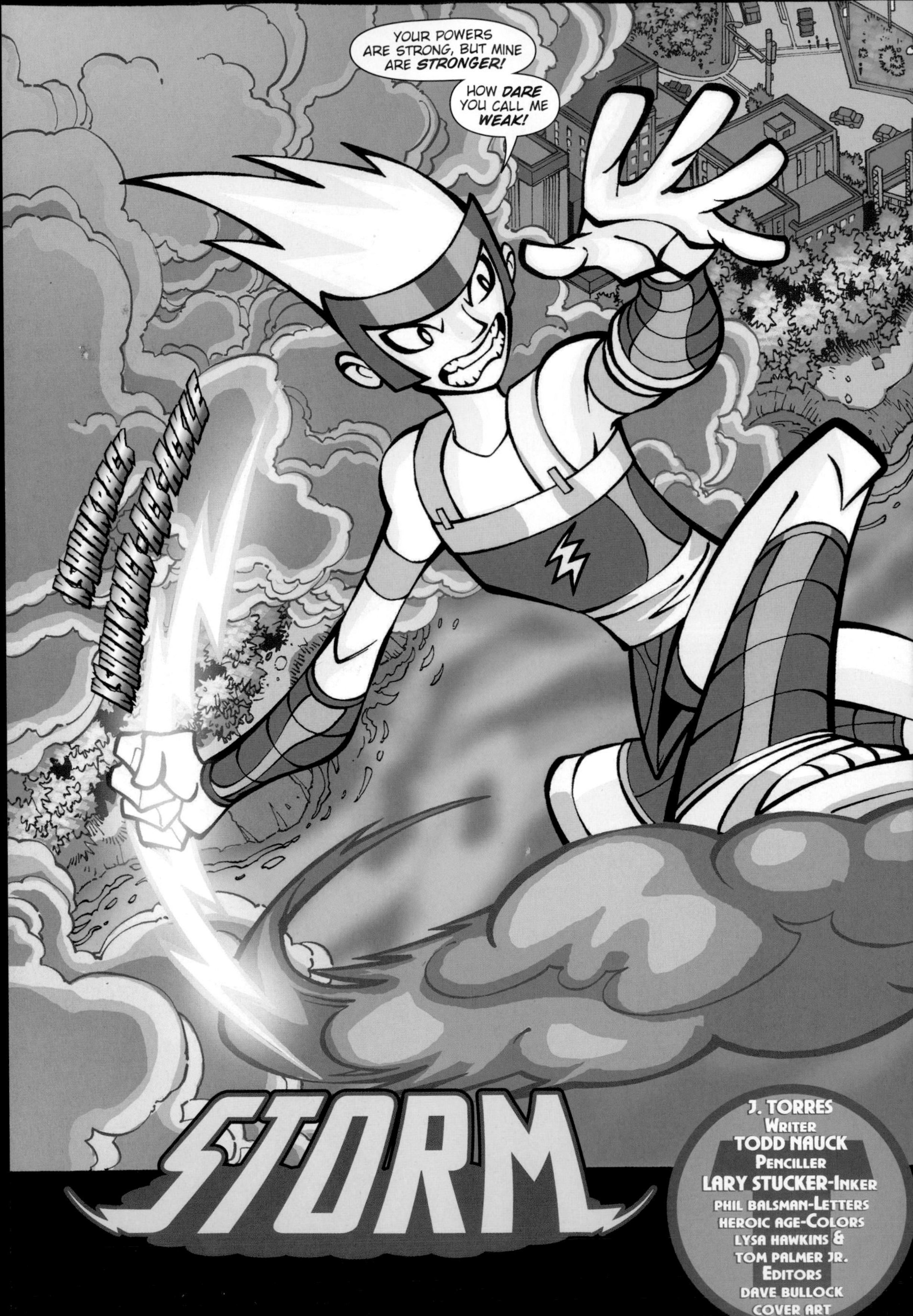
YOUR POWERS ARE STRONG, BUT MINE ARE STRONGER!
HOW DARE YOU CALL ME WEAK!
STORM
J. TORRES Writer
TODD NAUCK Penciller
LARY STUCKER-Inker
PHIL BALSMAN-Letters
HEROIC AGE-Colors
LYSA HAWKINS & TOM PALMER JR. Editors
DAVE BULLOCK COVER ART

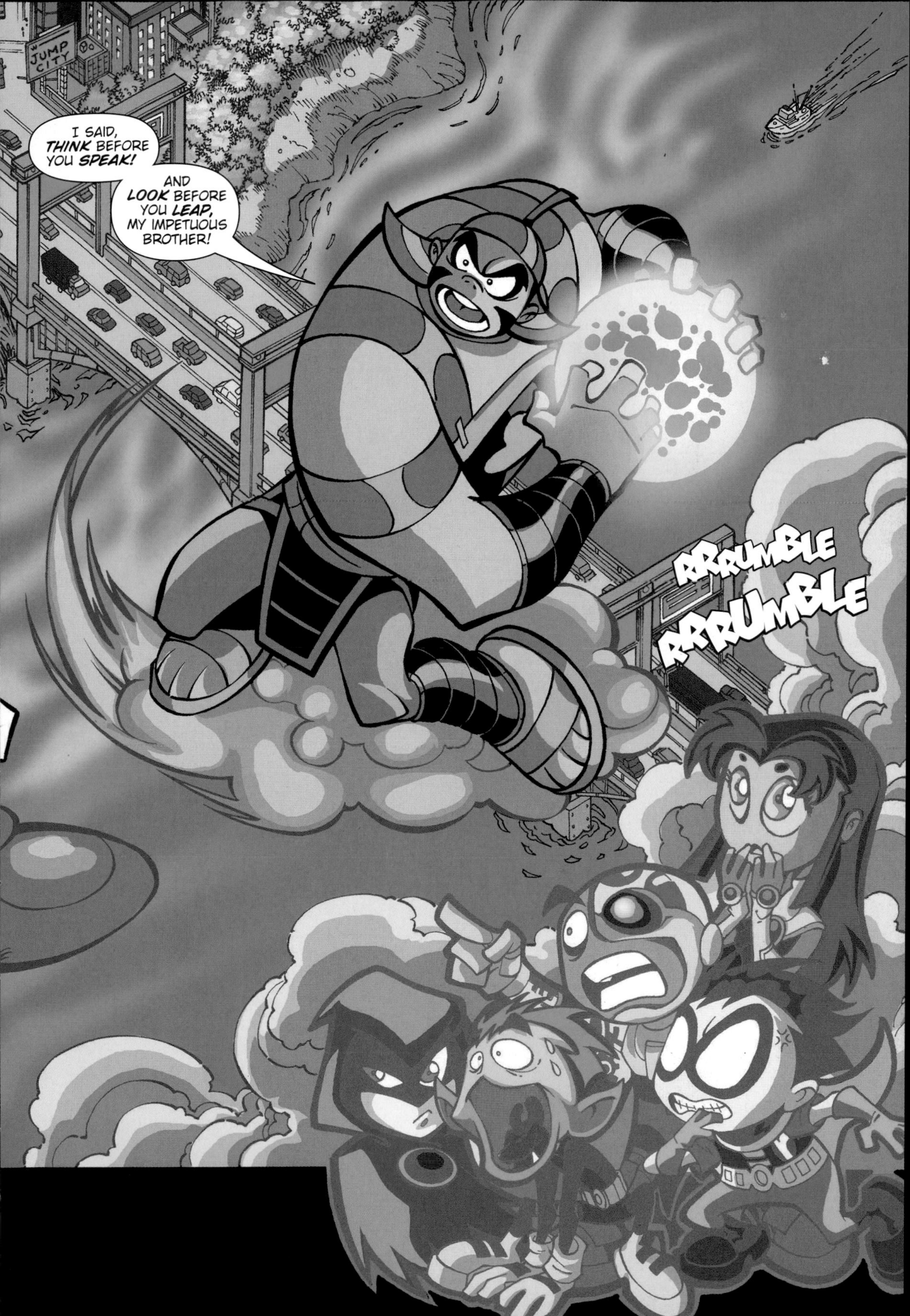
JUMP CITY
I SAID, THINK BEFORE YOU SPEAK!
AND LOOK BEFORE YOU LEAP, MY IMPETUOUS BROTHER!
RRRUMBLE
RRRUMBLE

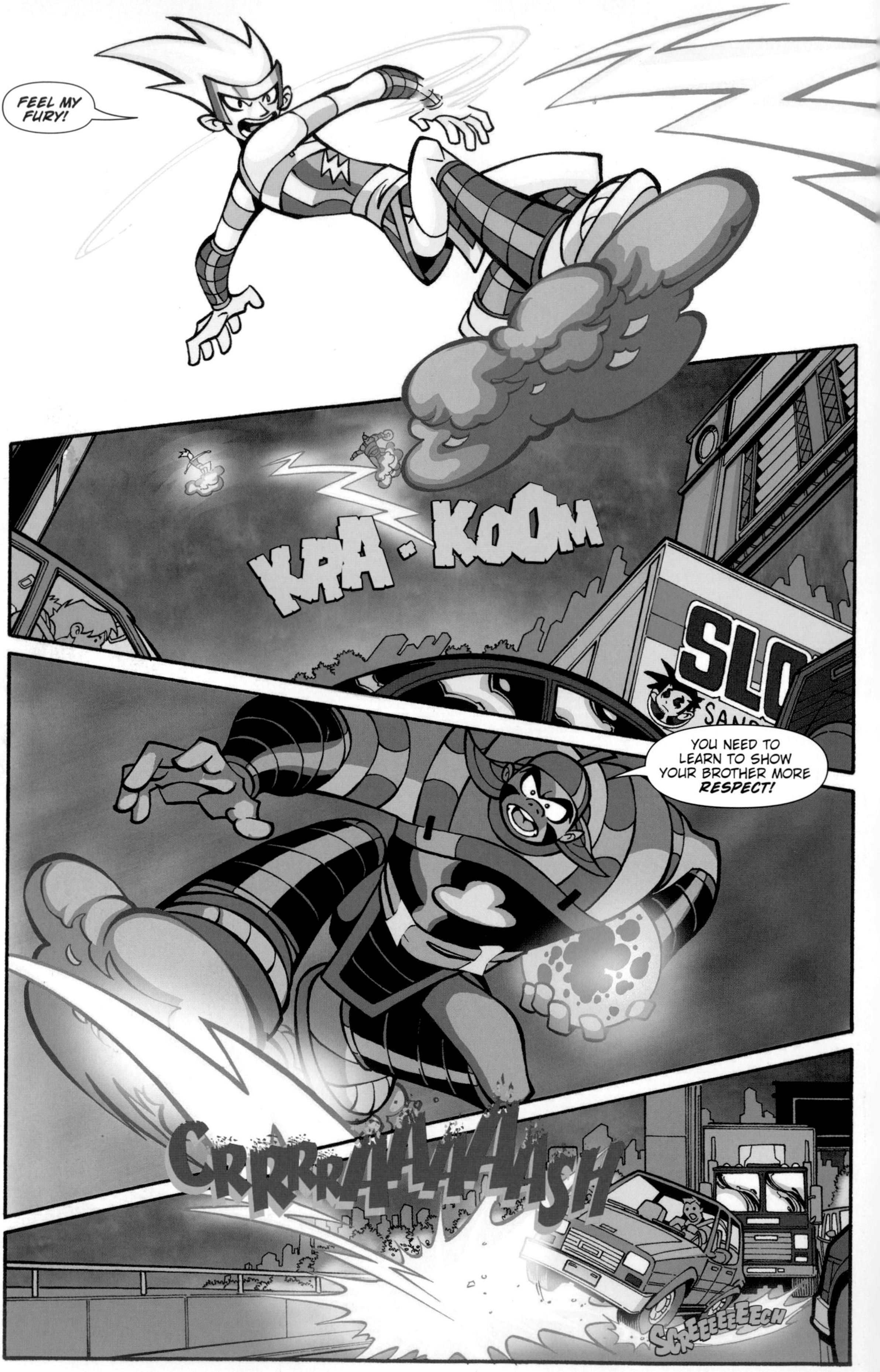
FEEL MY FURY!
KRA-KOOM
SLO
YOU NEED TO LEARN TO SHOW YOUR BROTHER MORE RESPECT!
CRRRRAAAAAASH
SCREEEEEEECH

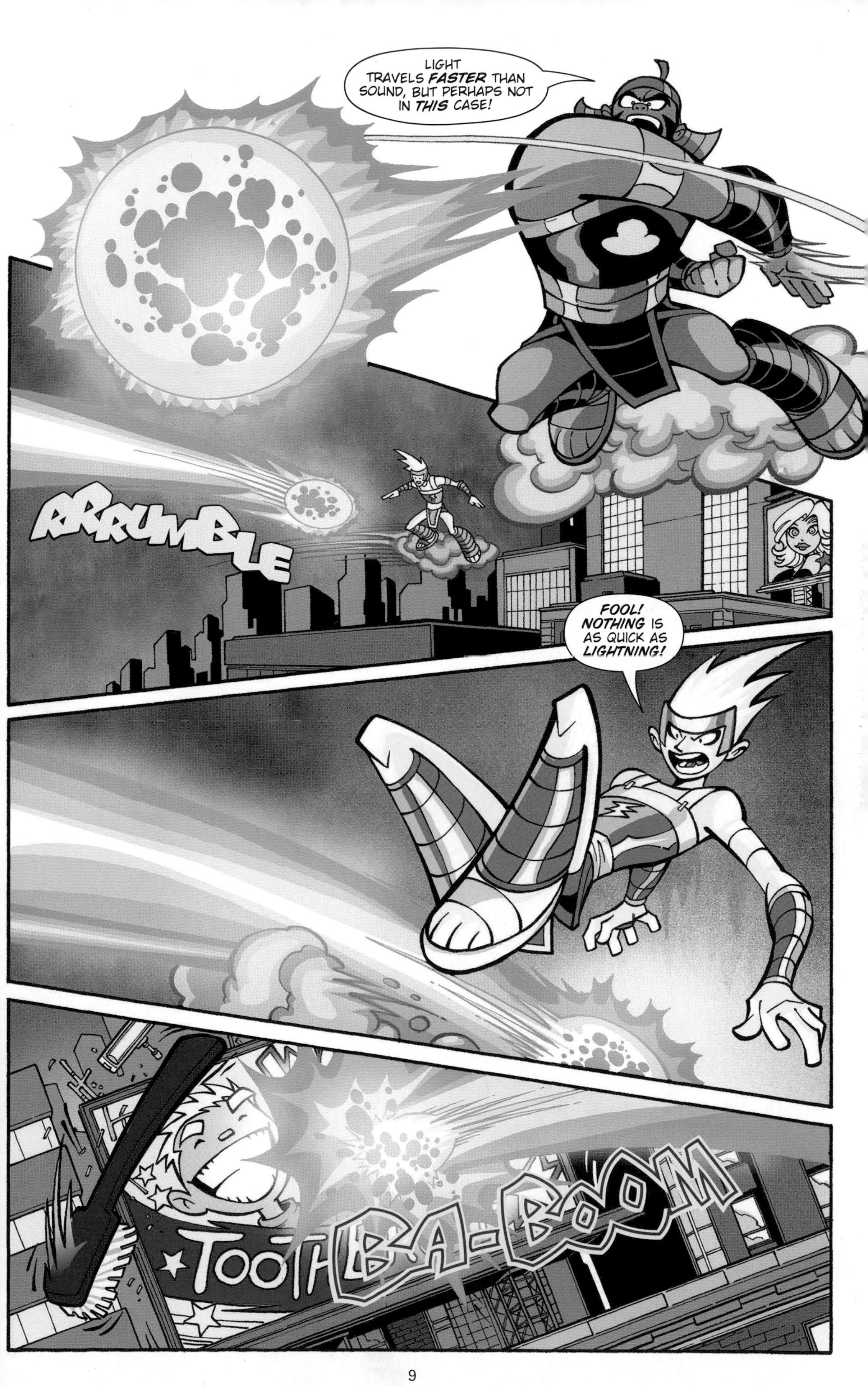
LIGHT TRAVELS FASTER THAN SOUND, BUT PERHAPS NOT IN THIS CASE!
RRRUMBLE
FOOL! NOTHING IS AS QUICK AS LIGHTNING!
TOOTH
BA-BOOM

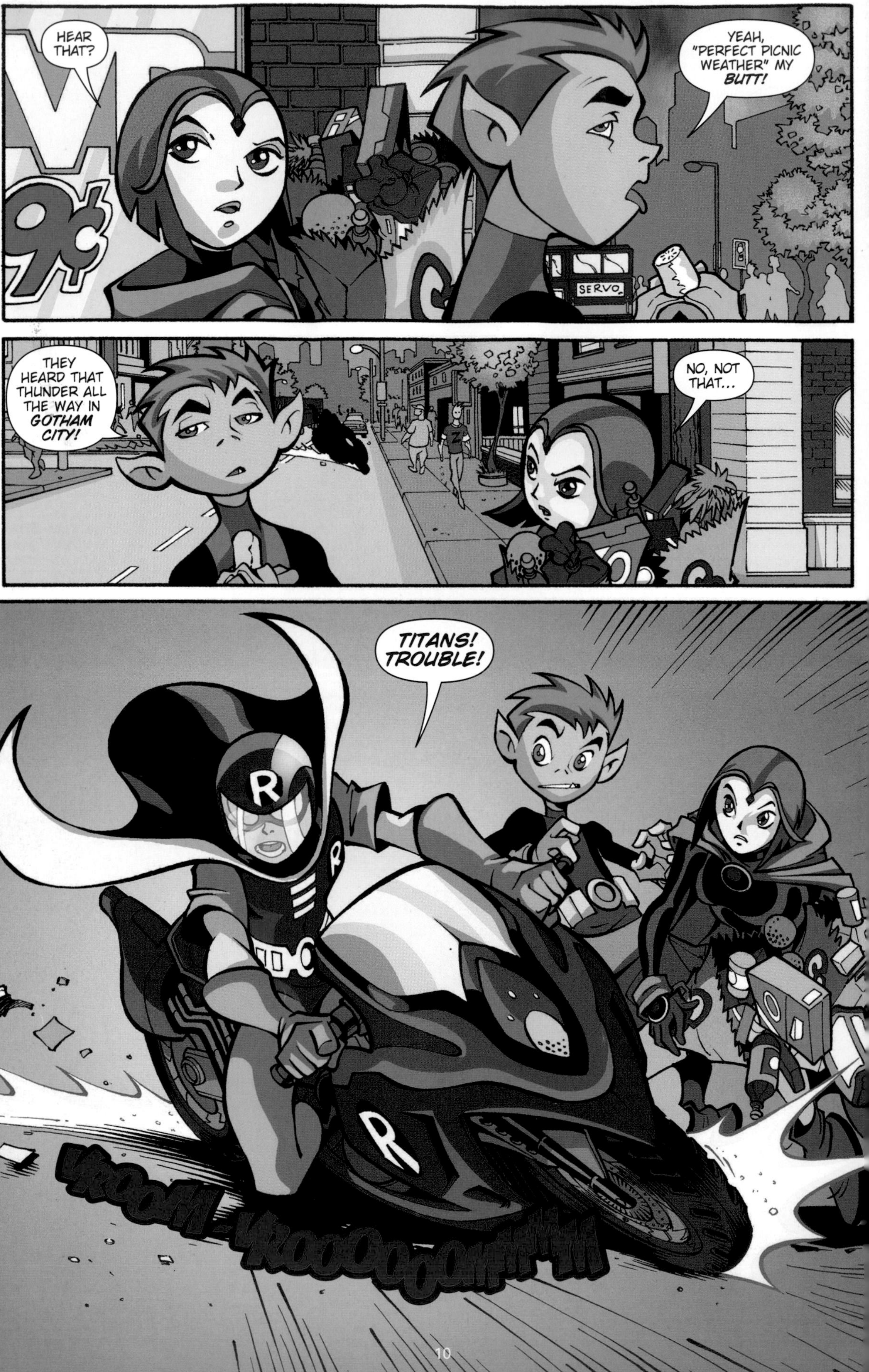
HEAR THAT?
YEAH, "PERFECT PICNIC WEATHER" MY BUTT!
SERVO
THEY HEARD THAT THUNDER ALL THE WAY IN GOTHAM CITY!
NO, NOT THAT...
TITANS! TROUBLE!
VROOM-VROOOOOOMMMMM

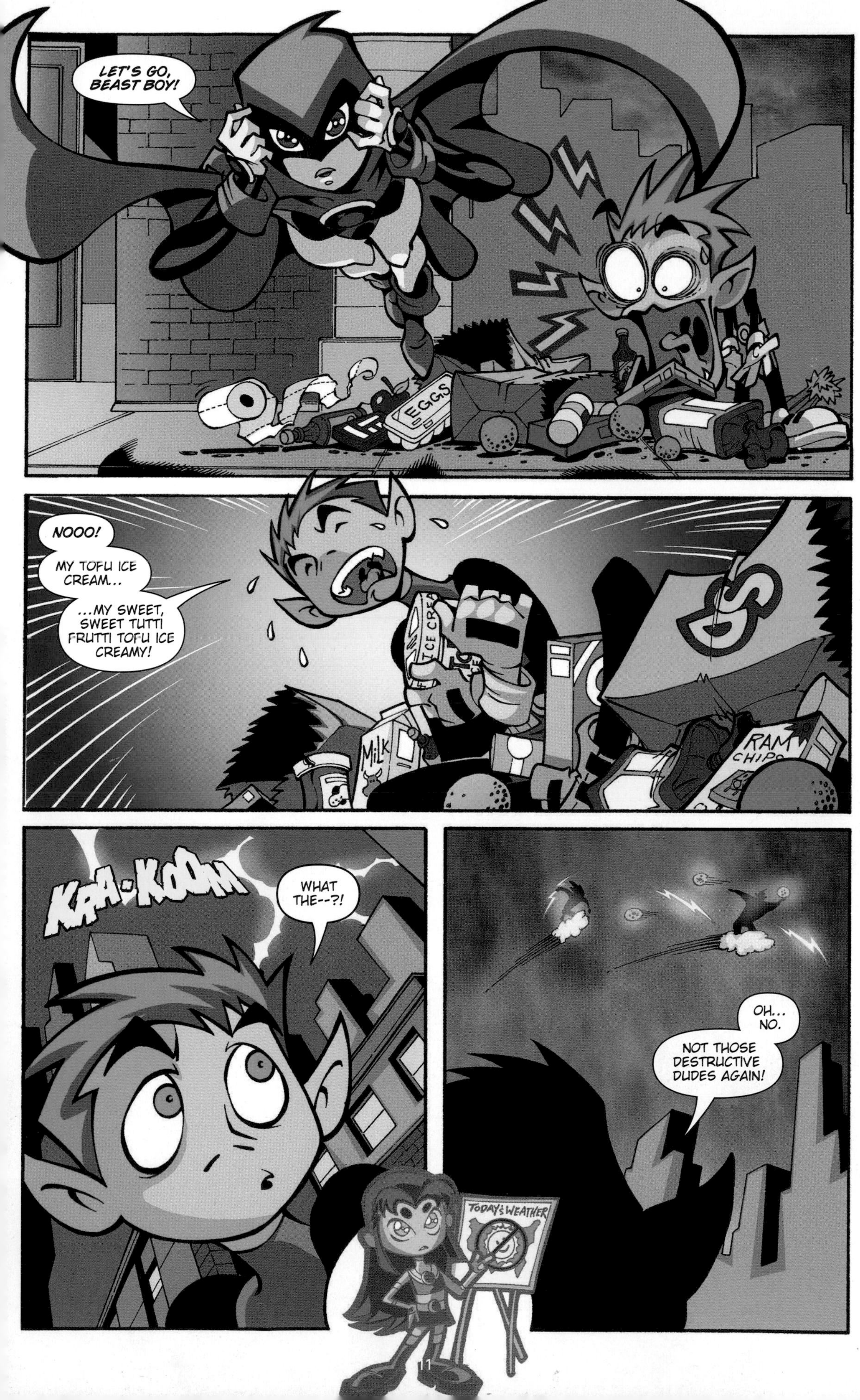
LET'S GO, BEAST BOY!
EGGS
NOOO!
MY TOFU ICE CREAM...
...MY SWEET, SWEET TUTTI FRUTTI TOFU ICE CREAMY!
MILK
RAM
CHIPS
KRA-KOOM
WHAT THE--?!
OH... NO.
NOT THOSE DESTRUCTIVE DUDES AGAIN!
TODAY'S WEATHER

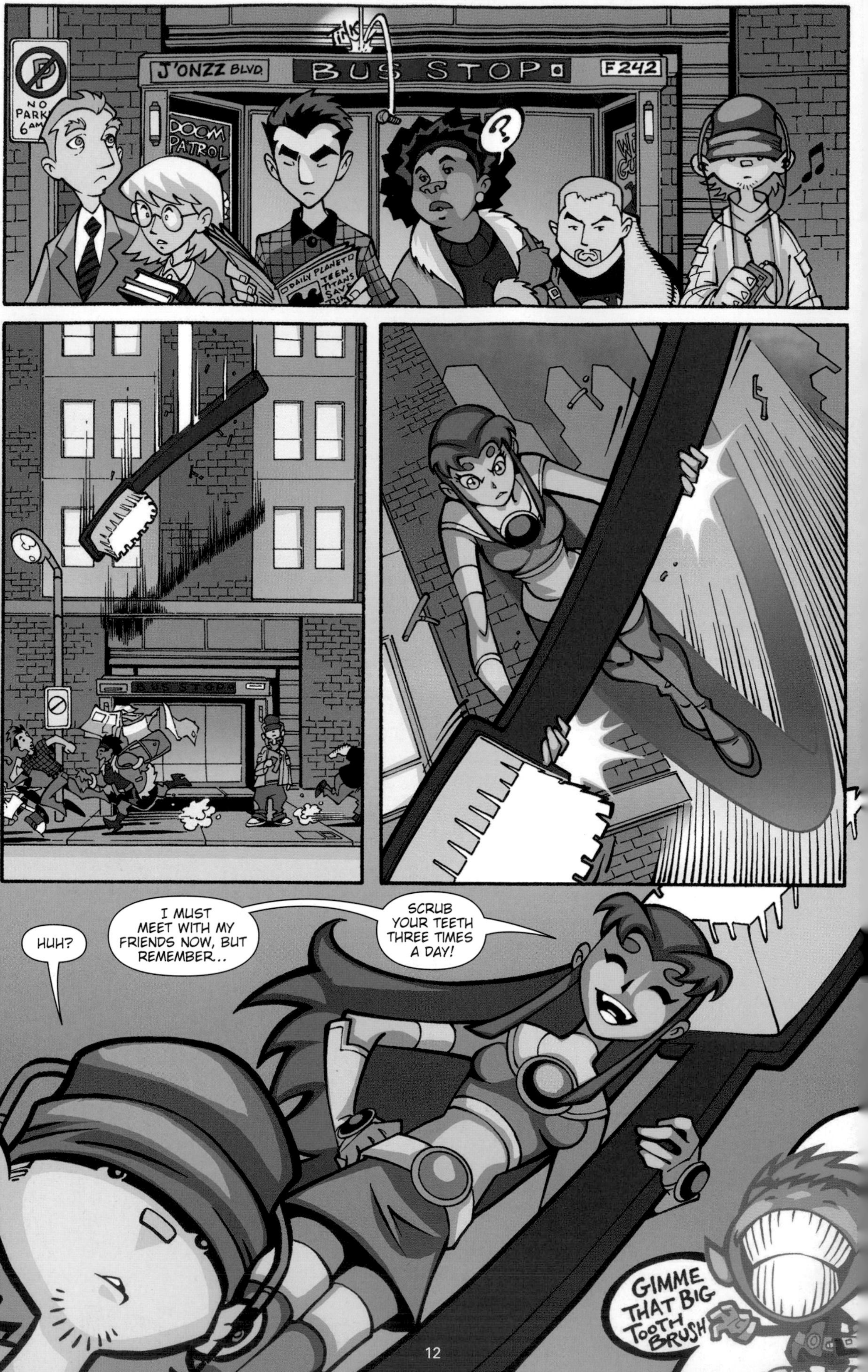
J'ONZZ BLVD.
BUS STOP
F242
NO PARK 6 AM
DOOM PATROL
?
DAILY PLANET TEEN TITANS SAVE
HUH?
I MUST MEET WITH MY FRIENDS NOW, BUT REMEMBER...
SCRUB YOUR TEETH THREE TIMES A DAY!
GIMME THAT BIG TOOTH BRUSH

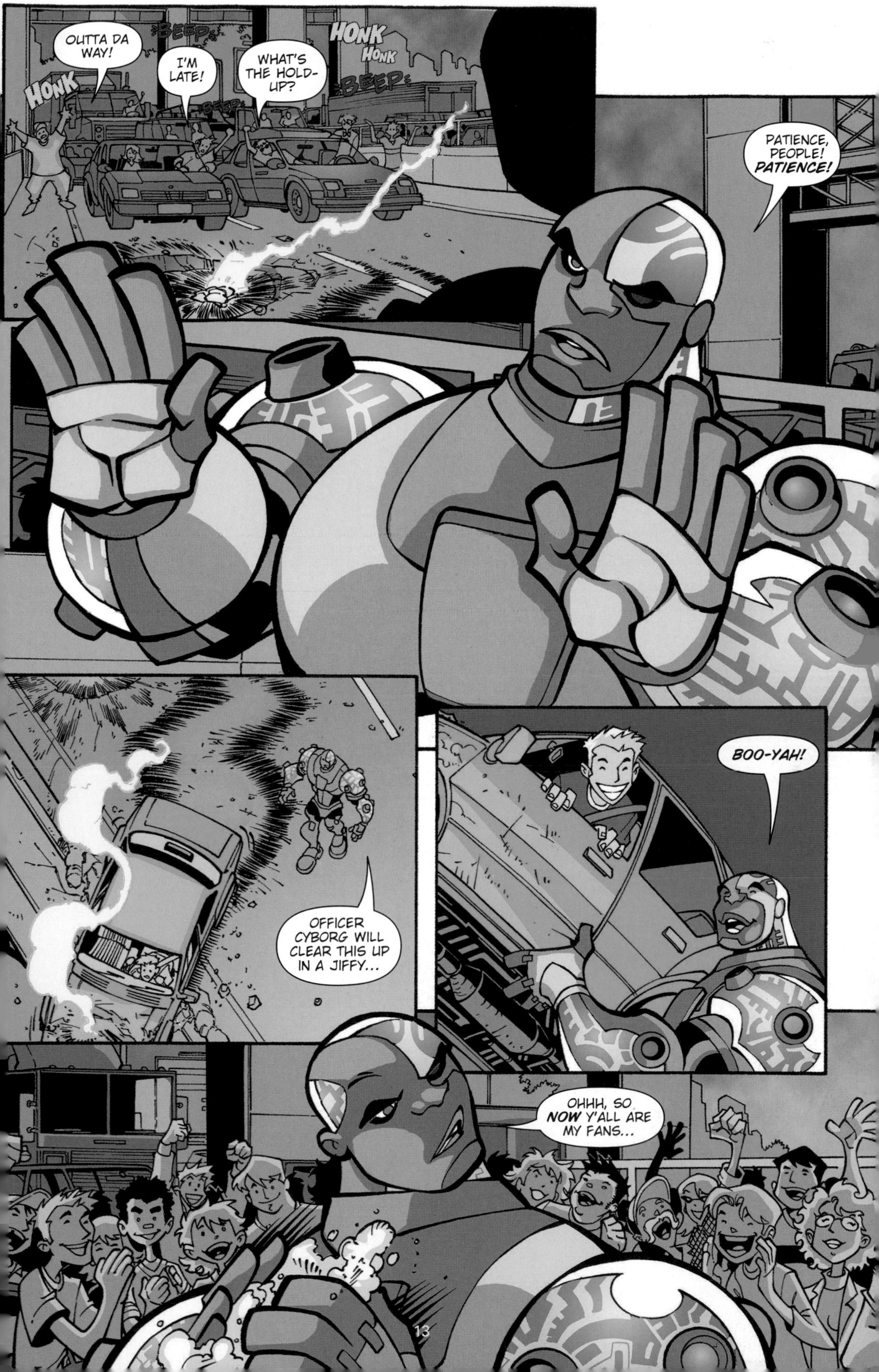
HONK
OUTTA DA WAY!
BEEP
I'M LATE!
BEEP
WHAT'S THE HOLD-UP?
HONK
HONK
BEEP
PATIENCE, PEOPLE! PATIENCE!
OFFICER CYBORG WILL CLEAR THIS UP IN A JIFFY...
BOO-YAH!
OHHH, SO NOW Y'ALL ARE MY FANS...

WELL, WELL, WELL. IF IT ISN'T *THUNDER* AND *LIGHTNING!*

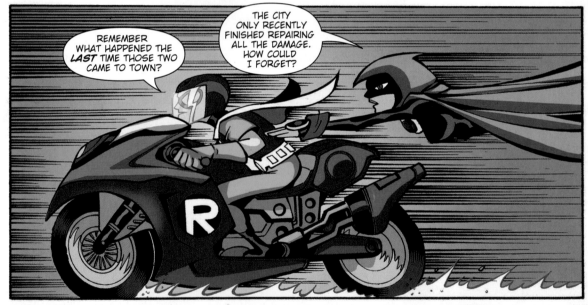

REMEMBER WHAT HAPPENED THE *LAST* TIME THOSE TWO CAME TO TOWN?

THE CITY ONLY RECENTLY FINISHED REPAIRING ALL THE DAMAGE. HOW COULD I FORGET?

THE BROTHERS WHO RIDE THE CLOUDS ARE ENGAGED IN A BATTLE WITH EACH OTHER?!

TURN AND FACE ME, COWARD! *FINISH* WHAT YOU STARTED!

WHAT *I* STARTED? *YOU* WERE THE FIRST TO STRIKE, *LIGHTNING!*

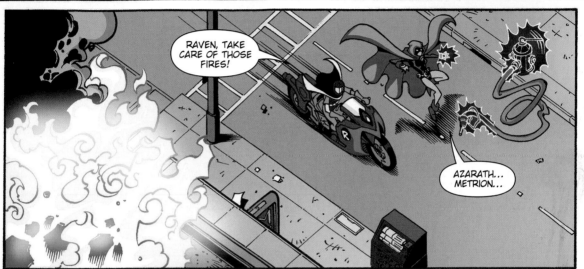

RAVEN, TAKE CARE OF THOSE FIRES!

AZARATH... METRION...

ZINTHOS!

ONE OF YOU GUYS GET UP THERE AND *STOP* THOSE TWO BEFORE THEY *KILL* EACH OTHER...

WHAT WOULD YOU CALL ROBIN...

IF HE WERE LIGHTNING'S BROTHER?

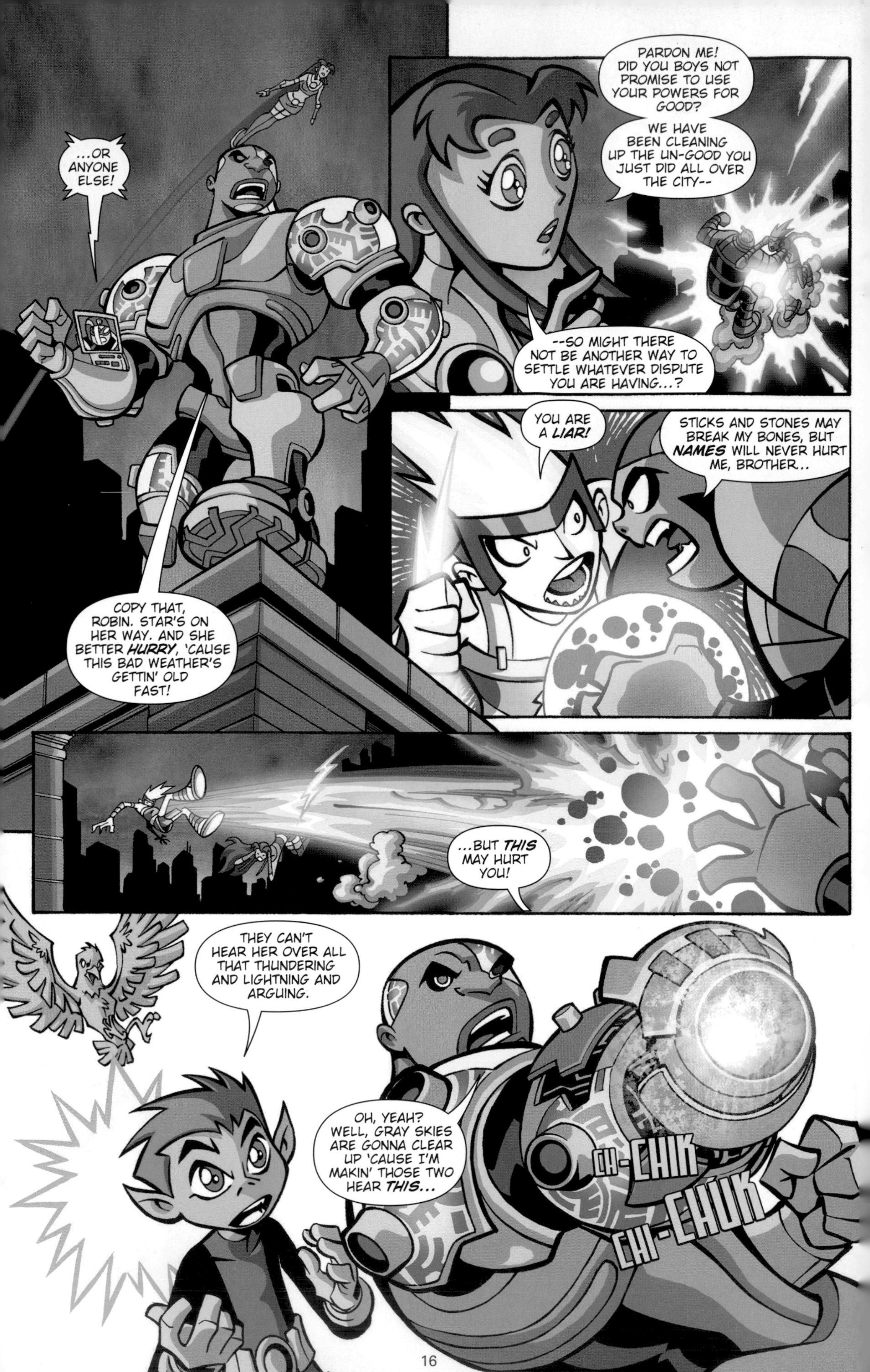
...OR ANYONE ELSE!
PARDON ME! DID YOU BOYS NOT PROMISE TO USE YOUR POWERS FOR GOOD?
WE HAVE BEEN CLEANING UP THE UN-GOOD YOU JUST DID ALL OVER THE CITY--
--SO MIGHT THERE NOT BE ANOTHER WAY TO SETTLE WHATEVER DISPUTE YOU ARE HAVING...?
COPY THAT, ROBIN. STAR'S ON HER WAY. AND SHE BETTER HURRY, 'CAUSE THIS BAD WEATHER'S GETTIN' OLD FAST!
YOU ARE A LIAR!
STICKS AND STONES MAY BREAK MY BONES, BUT NAMES WILL NEVER HURT ME, BROTHER...
...BUT THIS MAY HURT YOU!
THEY CAN'T HEAR HER OVER ALL THAT THUNDERING AND LIGHTNING AND ARGUING.
OH, YEAH? WELL, GRAY SKIES ARE GONNA CLEAR UP 'CAUSE I'M MAKIN' THOSE TWO HEAR THIS...
CH-CHIK
CH-CHUK

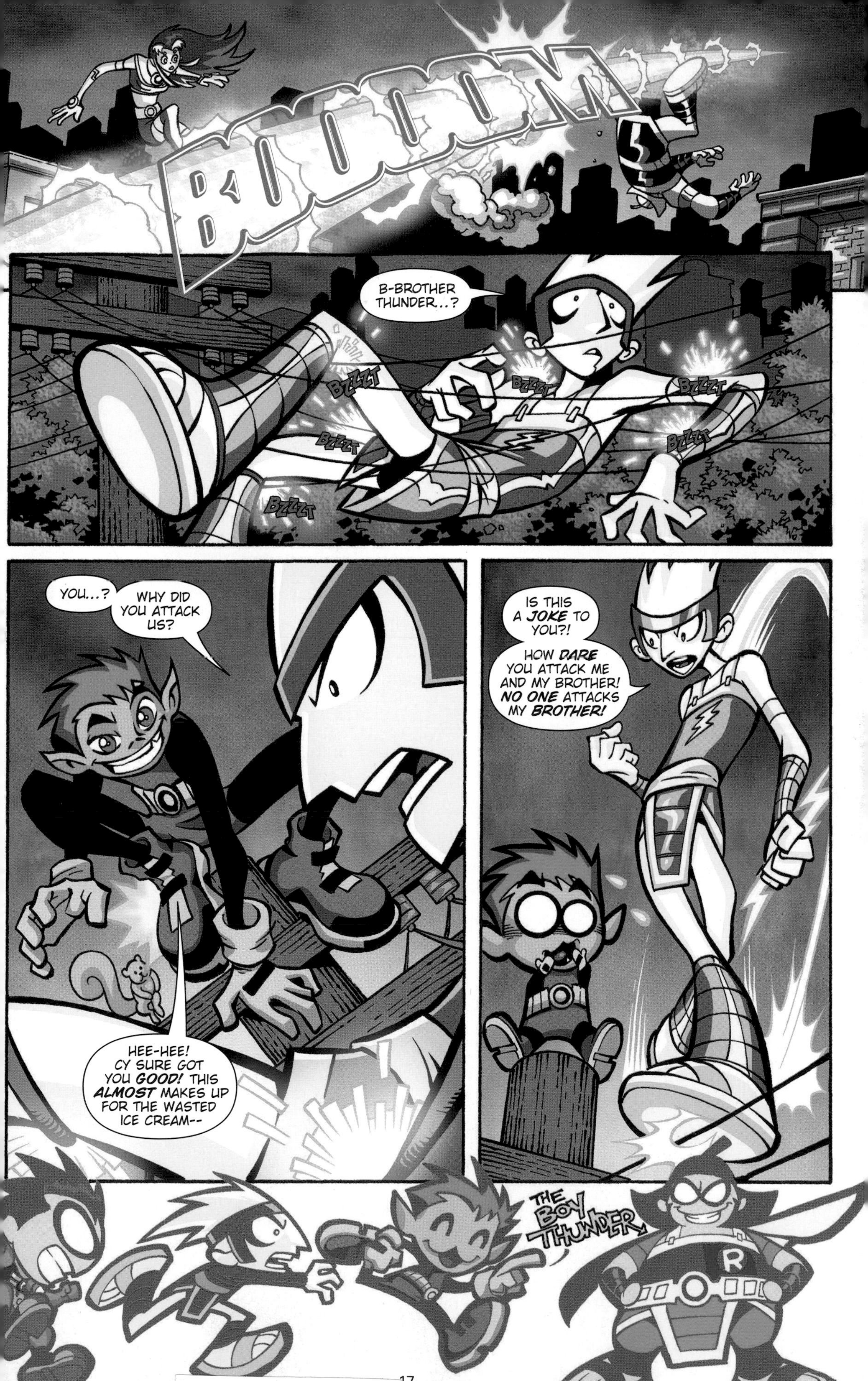
BOOOOM
B-BROTHER THUNDER...?
BZZZZT
BZZZZT
BZZZZT
BZZZZT
BZZZZT
YOU...?
WHY DID YOU ATTACK US?
HEE-HEE! CY SURE GOT YOU **GOOD!** THIS ***ALMOST*** MAKES UP FOR THE WASTED ICE CREAM--
IS THIS A ***JOKE*** TO YOU?!
HOW ***DARE*** YOU ATTACK ME AND MY BROTHER! ***NO ONE*** ATTACKS MY ***BROTHER!***
THE BOY THUNDER

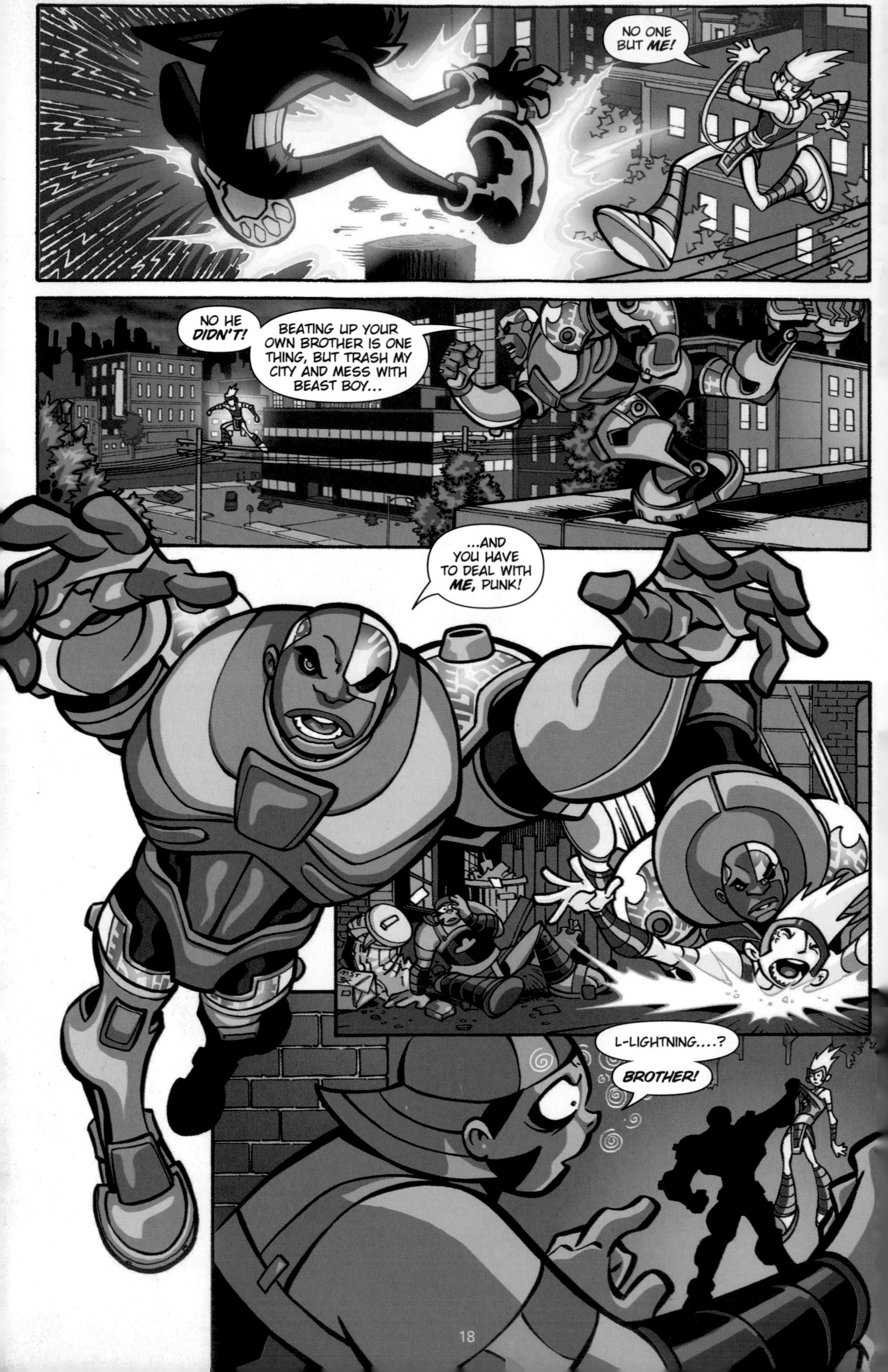
NO ONE BUT ME!
NO HE DIDN'T!
BEATING UP YOUR OWN BROTHER IS ONE THING, BUT TRASH MY CITY AND MESS WITH BEAST BOY...
...AND YOU HAVE TO DEAL WITH ME, PUNK!
L-LIGHTNING....?
BROTHER!

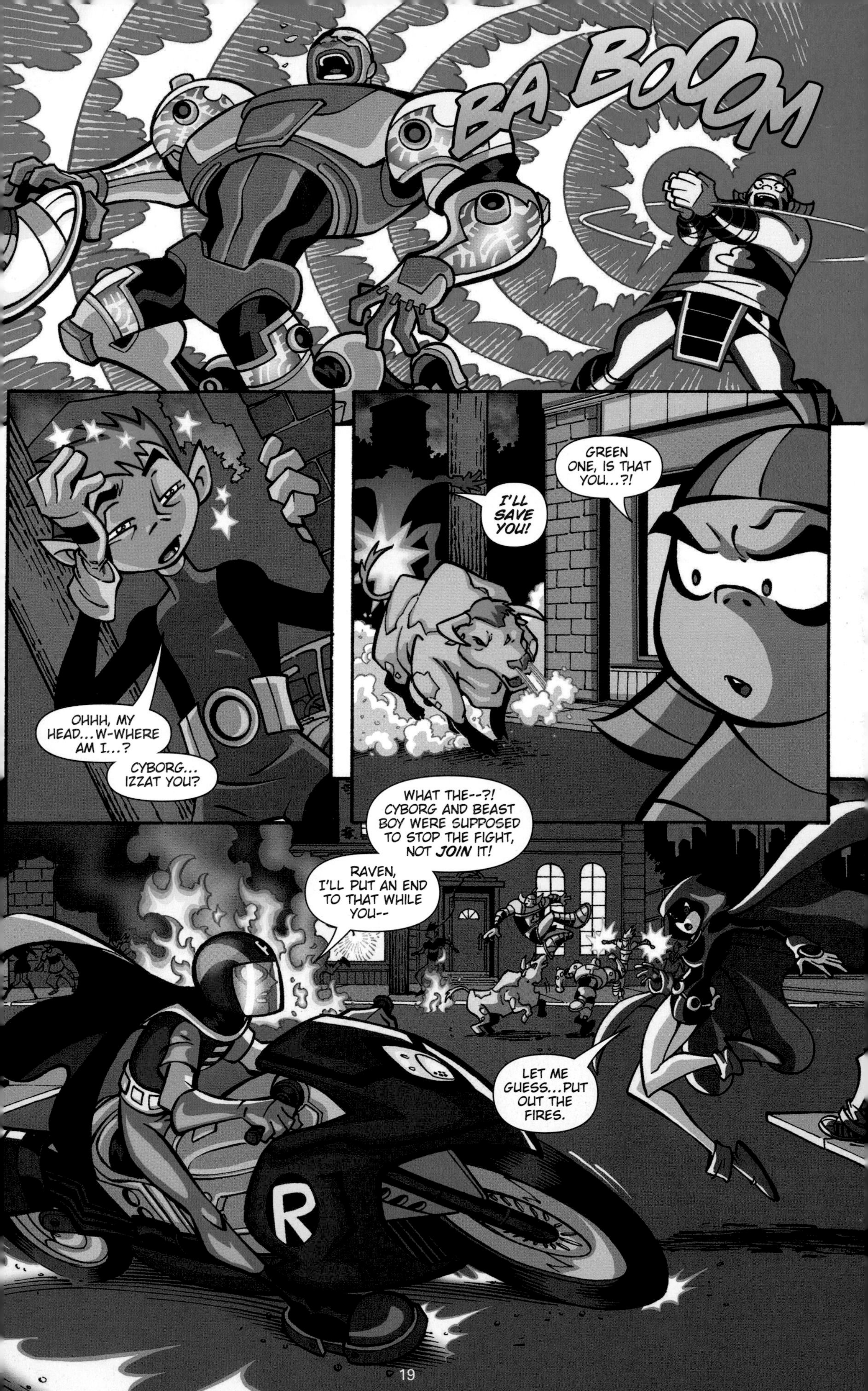
BA BOOOM
OHHH, MY HEAD...W-WHERE AM I...?
CYBORG... IZZAT YOU?
I'LL SAVE YOU!
GREEN ONE, IS THAT YOU...?!
WHAT THE--?! CYBORG AND BEAST BOY WERE SUPPOSED TO STOP THE FIGHT, NOT JOIN IT!
RAVEN, I'LL PUT AN END TO THAT WHILE YOU--
LET ME GUESS...PUT OUT THE FIRES.
R

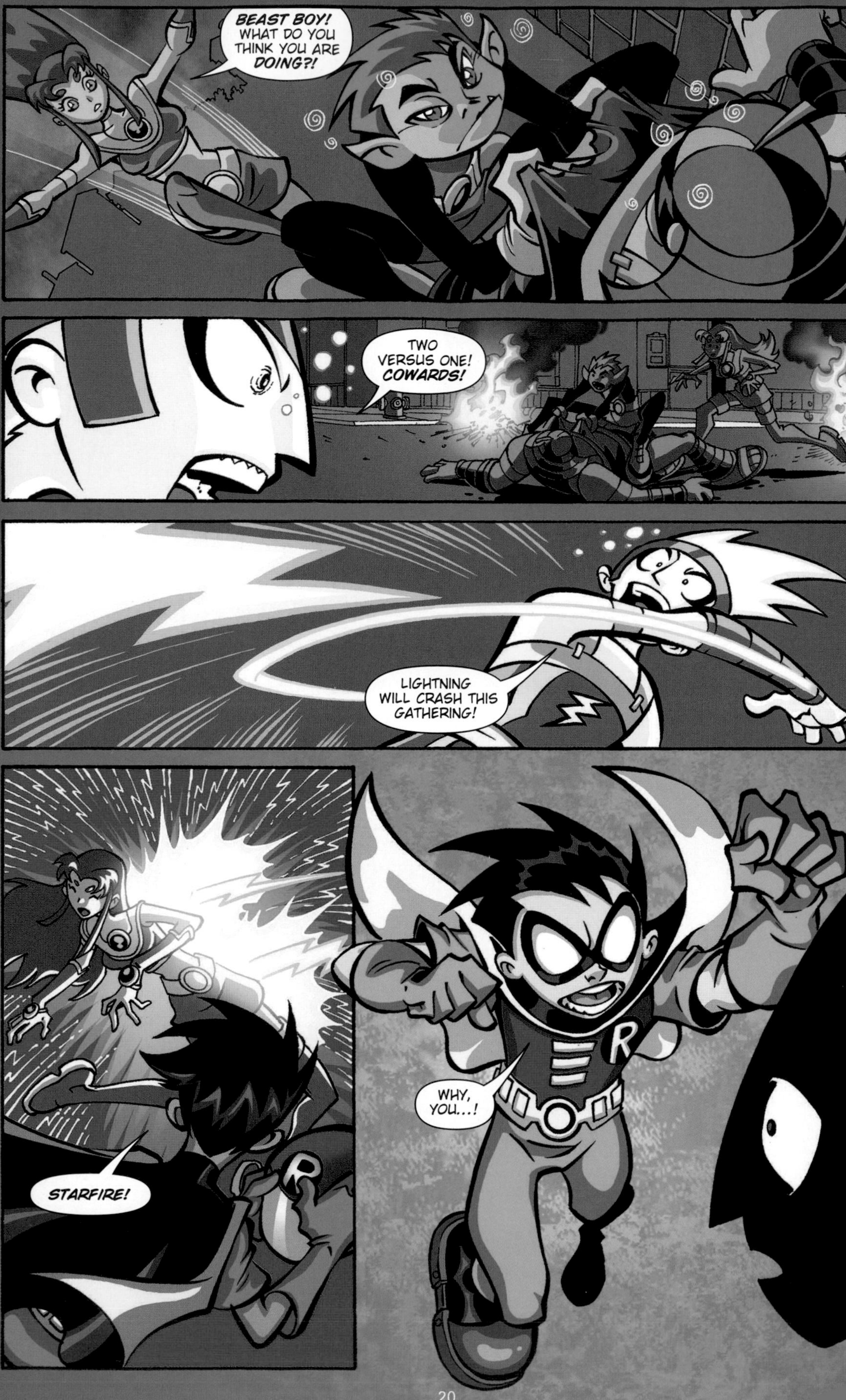
BEAST BOY! WHAT DO YOU THINK YOU ARE DOING?!
TWO VERSUS ONE! COWARDS!
LIGHTNING WILL CRASH THIS GATHERING!
STARFIRE!
WHY, YOU...!

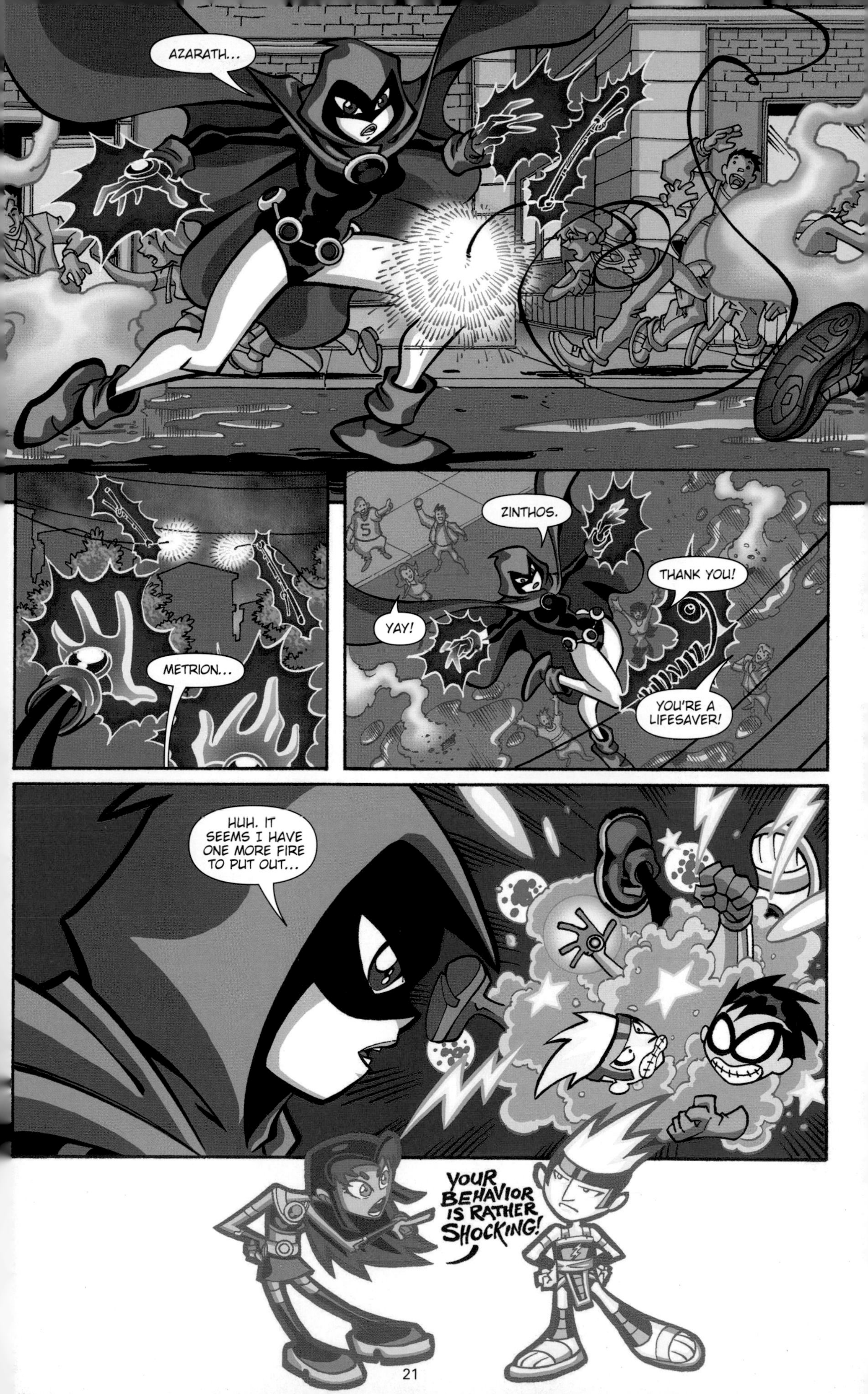
AZARATH...
METRION...
ZINTHOS.
YAY!
THANK YOU!
YOU'RE A LIFESAVER!
HUH. IT SEEMS I HAVE ONE MORE FIRE TO PUT OUT...
YOUR BEHAVIOR IS RATHER SHOCKING!

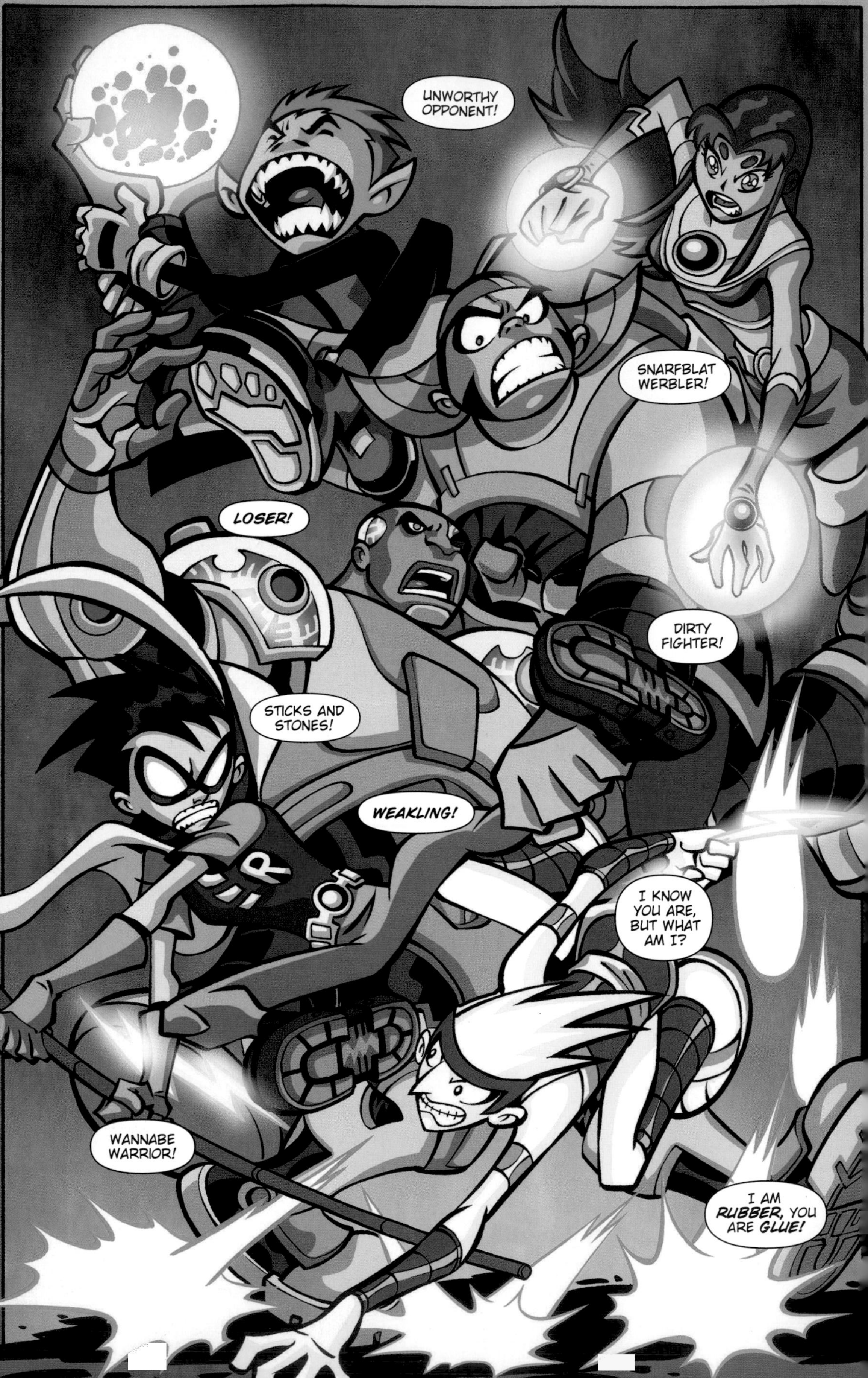
UNWORTHY OPPONENT!
SNARFBLAT WERBLER!
LOSER!
DIRTY FIGHTER!
STICKS AND STONES!
WEAKLING!
I KNOW YOU ARE, BUT WHAT AM I?
WANNABE WARRIOR!
I AM RUBBER, YOU ARE GLUE!

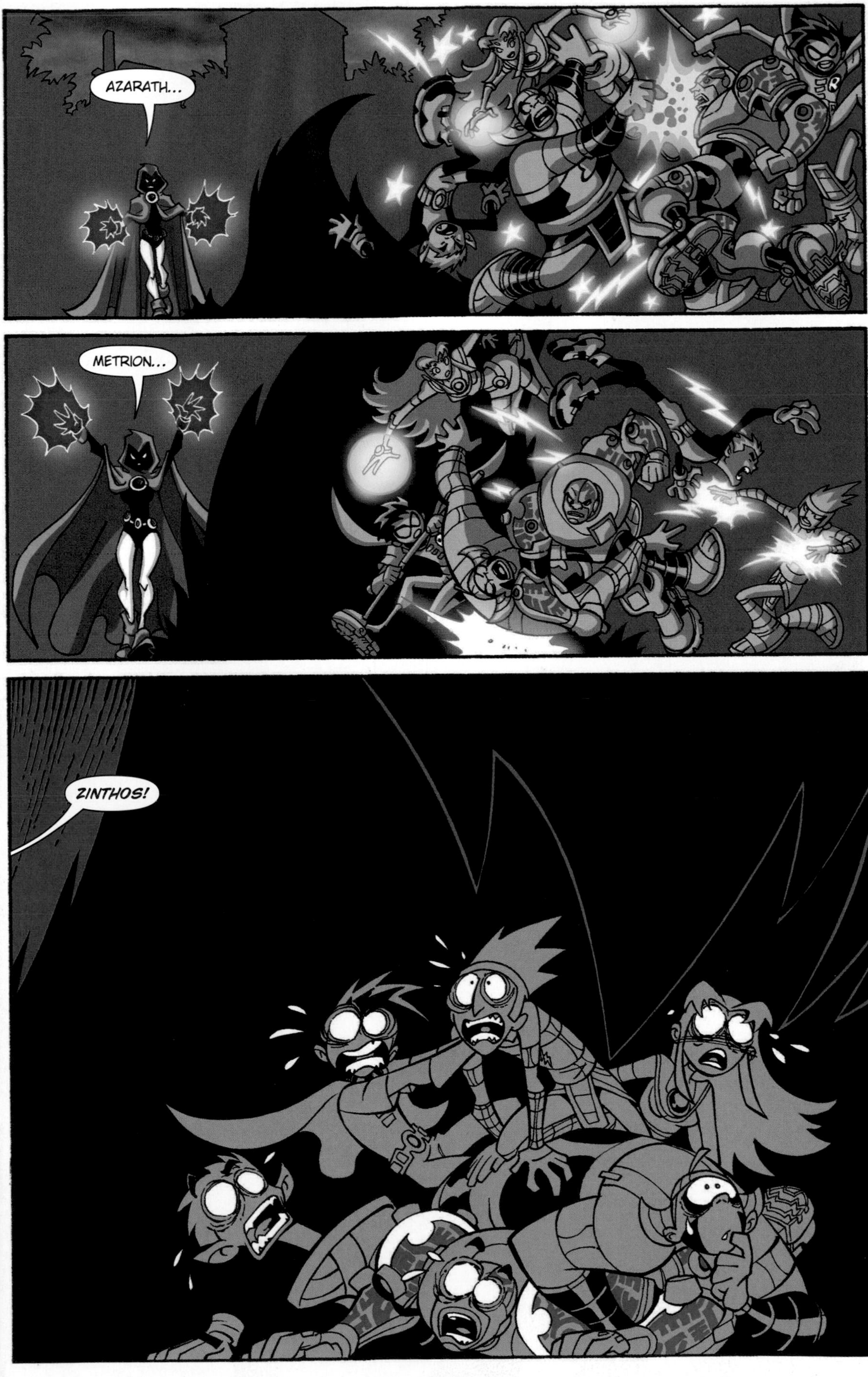
AZARATH...
METRION...
ZINTHOS!

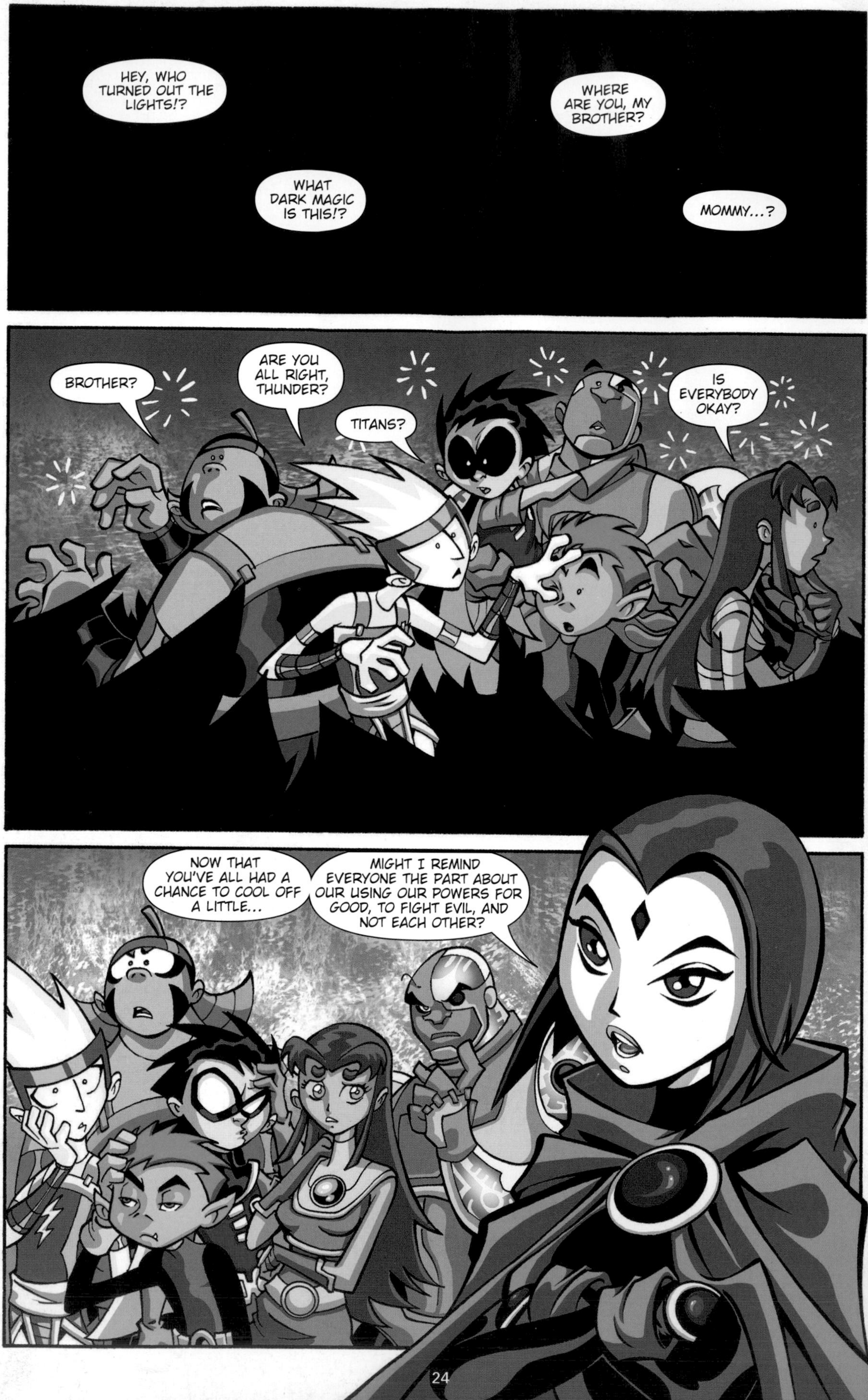
HEY, WHO TURNED OUT THE LIGHTS!?
WHAT DARK MAGIC IS THIS!?
WHERE ARE YOU, MY BROTHER?
MOMMY...?
BROTHER?
ARE YOU ALL RIGHT, THUNDER?
TITANS?
IS EVERYBODY OKAY?
NOW THAT YOU'VE ALL HAD A CHANCE TO COOL OFF A LITTLE...
MIGHT I REMIND EVERYONE THE PART ABOUT OUR USING OUR POWERS FOR GOOD, TO FIGHT EVIL, AND NOT EACH OTHER?

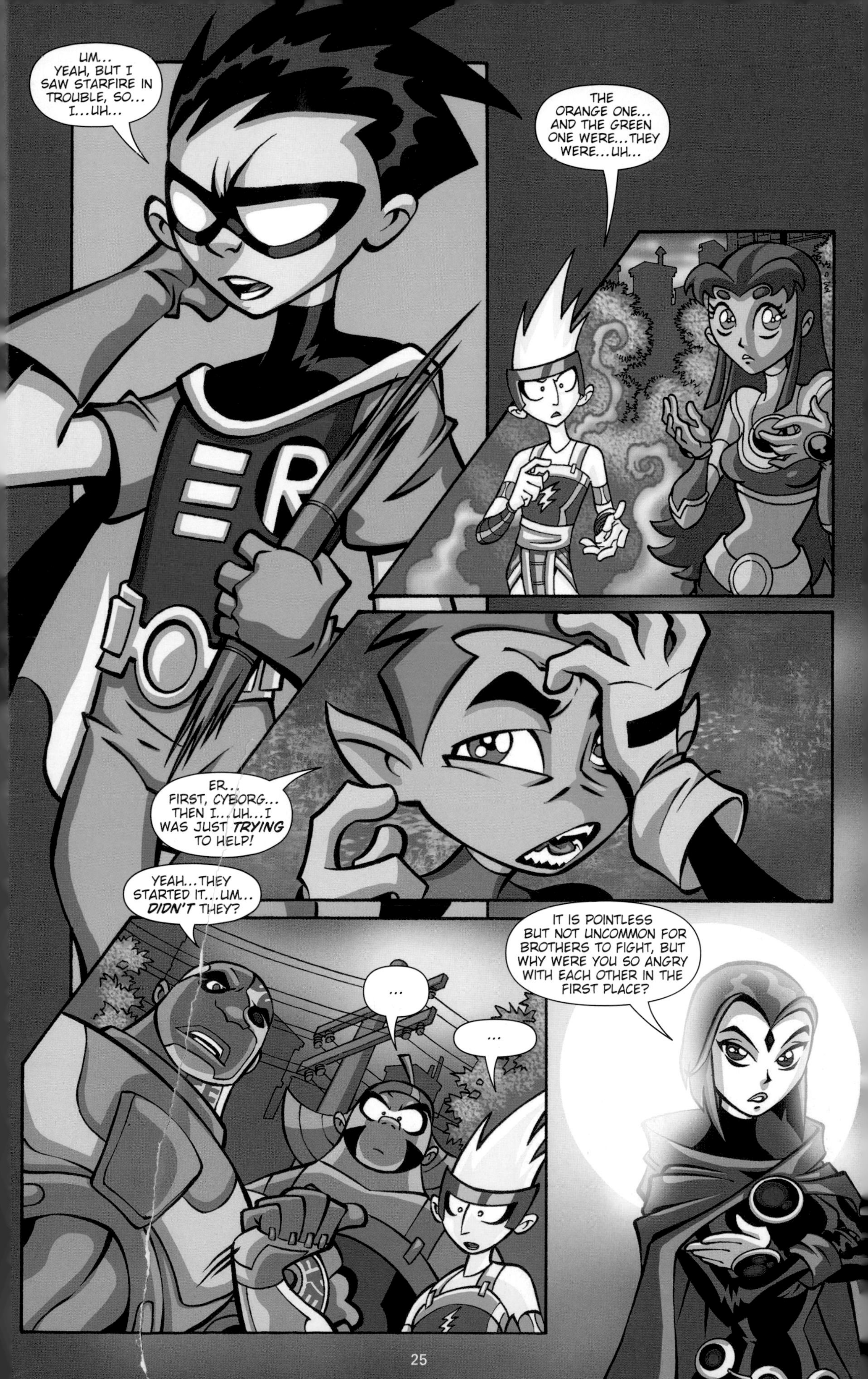
UM... YEAH, BUT I SAW STARFIRE IN TROUBLE, SO... I...UH...
THE ORANGE ONE... AND THE GREEN ONE WERE...THEY WERE...UH...
ER.. FIRST, CYBORG... THEN I...UH...I WAS JUST *TRYING* TO HELP!
YEAH...THEY STARTED IT...UM... *DIDN'T* THEY?
...
...
IT IS POINTLESS BUT NOT UNCOMMON FOR BROTHERS TO FIGHT, BUT WHY WERE YOU SO ANGRY WITH EACH OTHER IN THE FIRST PLACE?

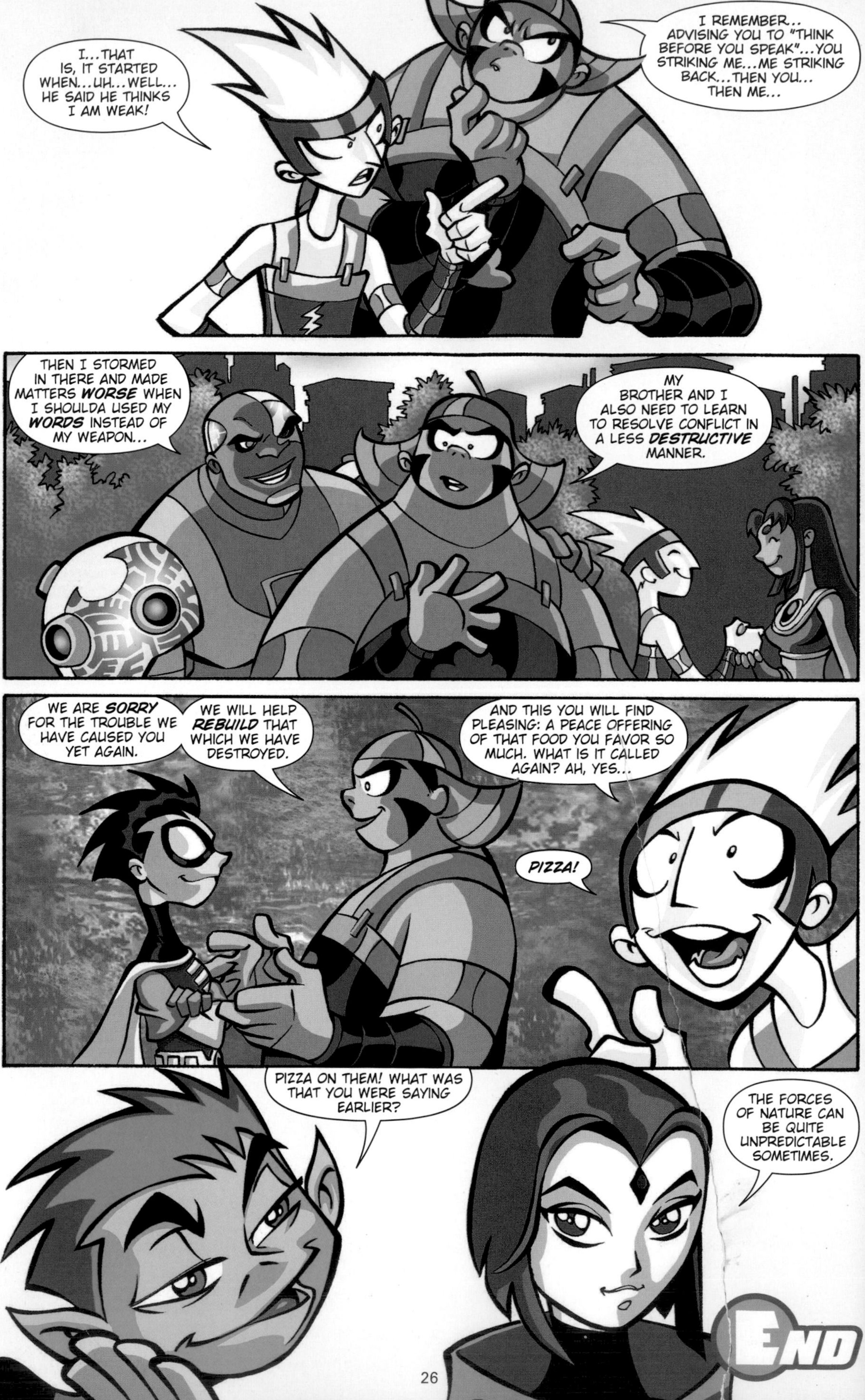
I...THAT IS, IT STARTED WHEN...UH...WELL... HE SAID HE THINKS I AM WEAK!
I REMEMBER... ADVISING YOU TO "THINK BEFORE YOU SPEAK"...YOU STRIKING ME...ME STRIKING BACK...THEN YOU... THEN ME...
THEN I STORMED IN THERE AND MADE MATTERS WORSE WHEN I SHOULDA USED MY WORDS INSTEAD OF MY WEAPON...
MY BROTHER AND I ALSO NEED TO LEARN TO RESOLVE CONFLICT IN A LESS DESTRUCTIVE MANNER.
WE ARE SORRY FOR THE TROUBLE WE HAVE CAUSED YOU YET AGAIN.
WE WILL HELP REBUILD THAT WHICH WE HAVE DESTROYED.
AND THIS YOU WILL FIND PLEASING: A PEACE OFFERING OF THAT FOOD YOU FAVOR SO MUCH. WHAT IS IT CALLED AGAIN? AH, YES...
PIZZA!
PIZZA ON THEM! WHAT WAS THAT YOU WERE SAYING EARLIER?
THE FORCES OF NATURE CAN BE QUITE UNPREDICTABLE SOMETIMES.
END

CREATORS

J. TORRES WRITER

J. Torres won the Shuster Award for Outstanding Writer for his work on Batman: Legends of the Dark Knight, Love As a Foreign Language, and Teen Titans Go! He is also the writer of the Eisner Award-nominated Alison Dare and the YALSA listed Days Like This and Lola: A Ghost Story. Other comic book credits include Avatar: The Last Airbender, Batman: The Brave and the Bold, Legion of Super-Heroes in the 31st Century, Ninja Scroll, Wonder Girl, Wonder Woman, and WALL-E: Recharge.

TODD NAUCK ARTIST

Todd Nauck is an American comic book artist and writer. Nauck is most notable for his work on Young Justice, Teen Titans Go!, and his own creation, Wildguard.

GLOSSARY

coward (COW-urd)--someone who is too afraid to do what is right or expected

destructive (di-STRUK-tiv)--causing a large amount of damage or harm

dispute (diss-PYOOT)--an argument, disagreement, or fight over something

engaged (en-GAYJD)--busy with some activity

force (FORSS)--power or violence

fury (FYOOR-ee)--violent anger, or a wild and dangerous force

impetuous (im-PETCH-oo-uhss)--controlled by emotion rather than thought

resolve (ri-ZALV)--to find an answer or solution to something

unpredictable (un-pre-DICT-uh-buhl)--unable to guess what someone or something might do

unworthy (un-WUHR-thee)--not deserving of respect, praise, or attention

weakling (WEAK-ling)--someone who is not strong and powerful

VISUAL QUESTIONS & PROMPTS

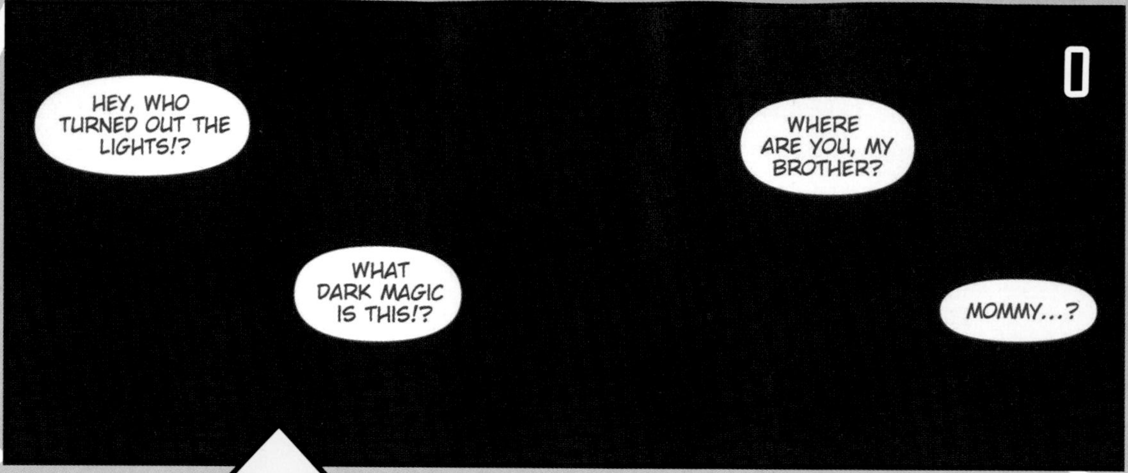
1
HEY, WHO TURNED OUT THE LIGHTS!?
WHERE ARE YOU, MY BROTHER?
WHAT DARK MAGIC IS THIS!?
MOMMY...?

1. Why did Raven decide to turn out the lights? What was her goal, and did it work?

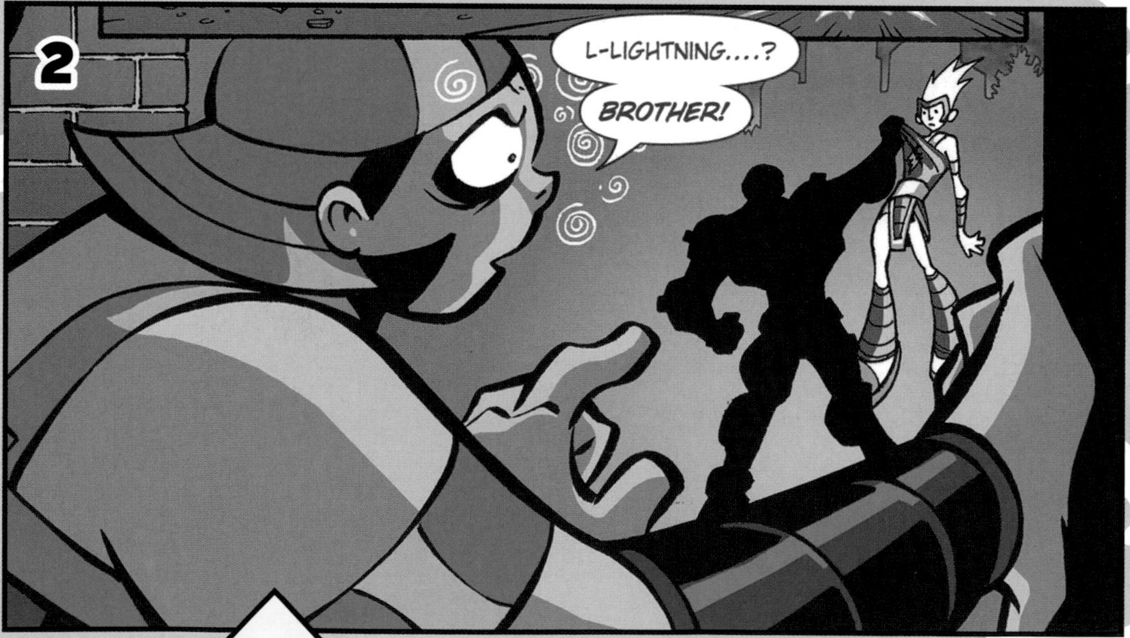
2
L-LIGHTNING....?
BROTHER!

2. What do the little swirls next to Thunder's head mean? How does he feel here?

3. The creators of this comic used sound effects, or SFX, to show noises. What are some other SFX that could've been used here?

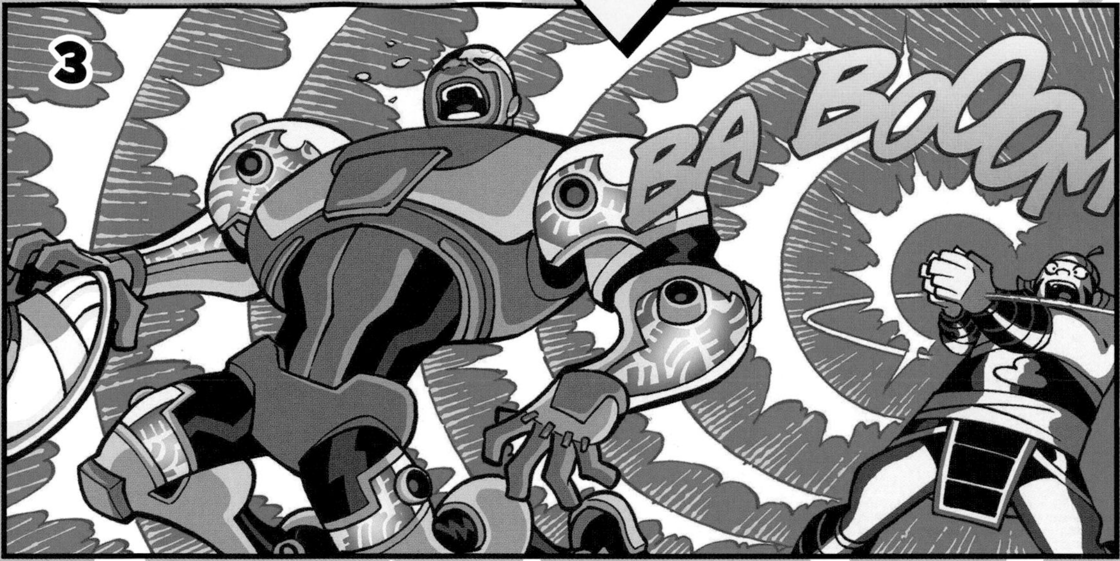
3
BA BOOOM

4. What do the little lightning bolts next to Beast Boy's head mean? How does he feel here--and why does he feel that way?

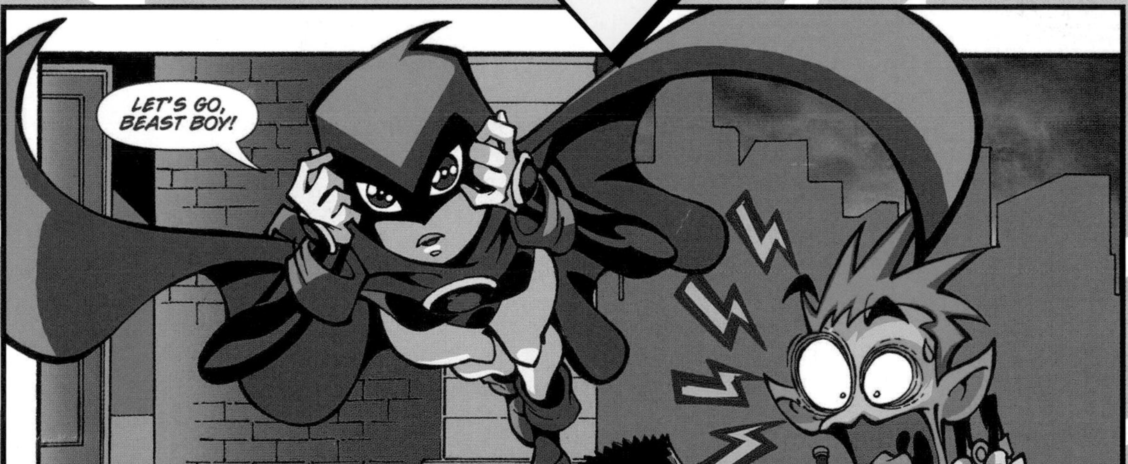
LET'S GO, BEAST BOY!
EGGS
4

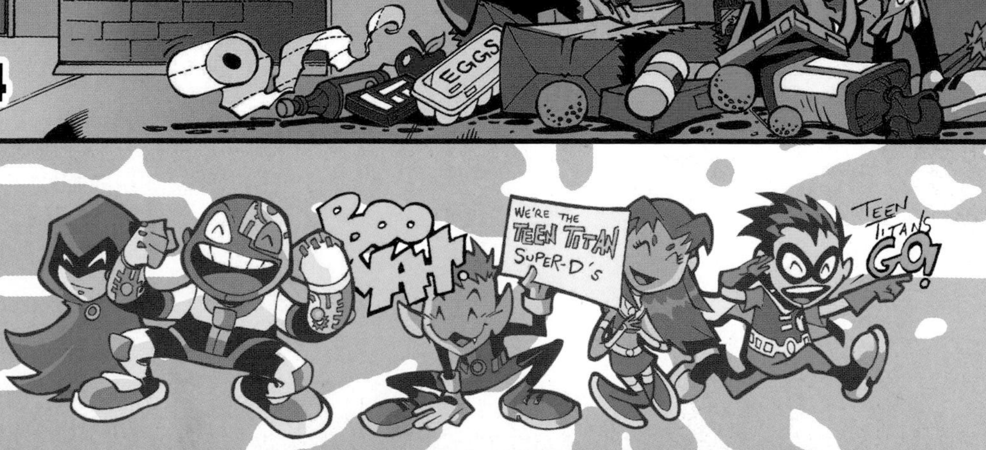
BOO YAH!
WE'RE THE TEEN TITAN SUPER-D'S
TEEN TITANS GO!

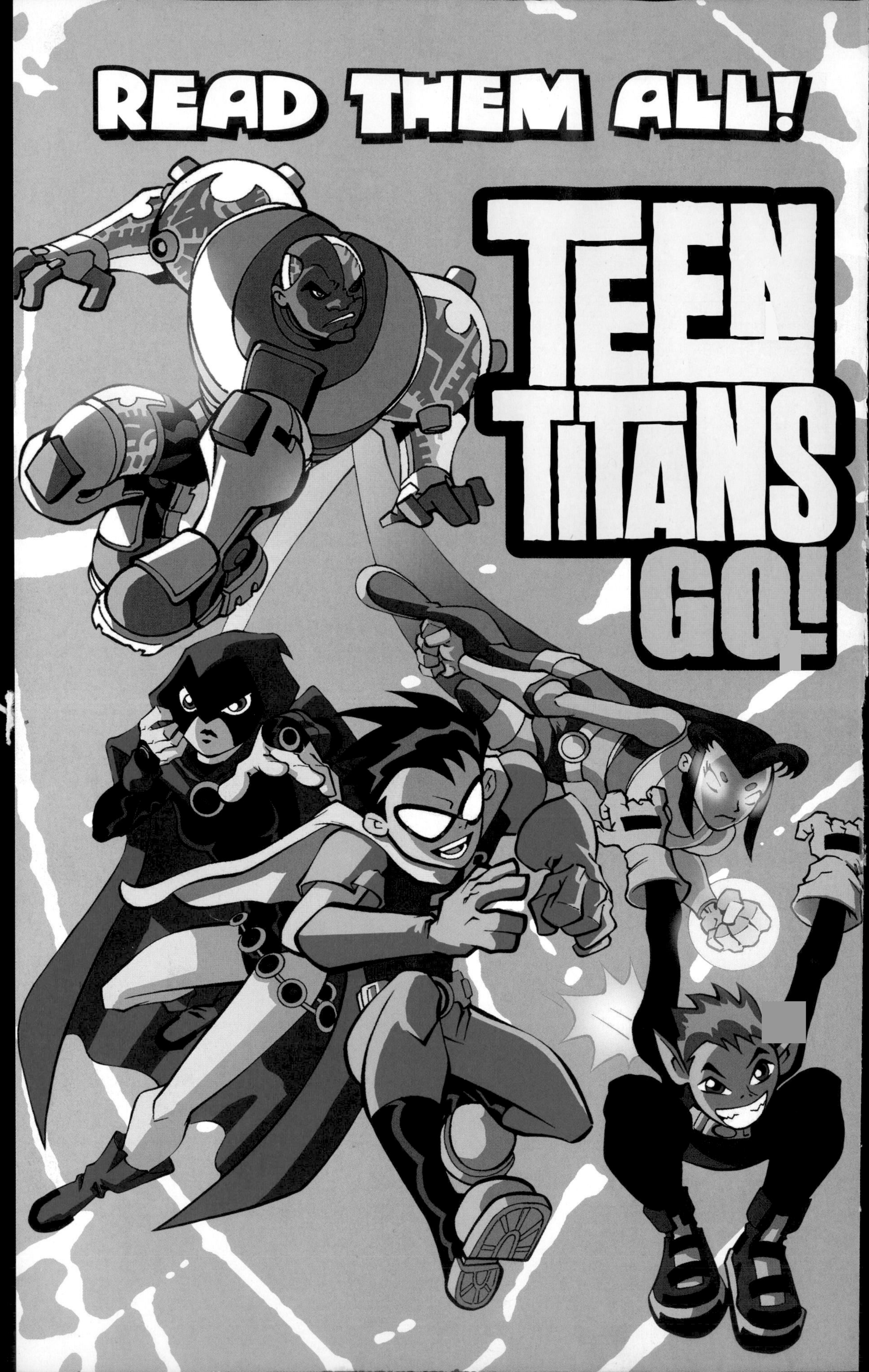
READ THEM ALL!
TEEN TITANS GO!

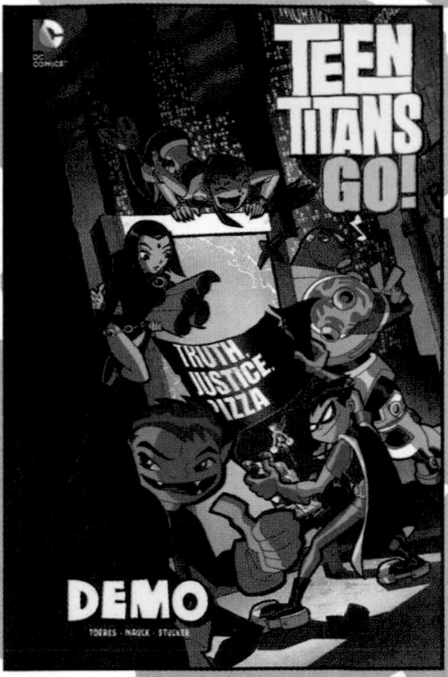
TEEN TITANS GO!
TRUTH JUSTICE PIZZA
DEMO
TORRES · MAUCK · STUCKER

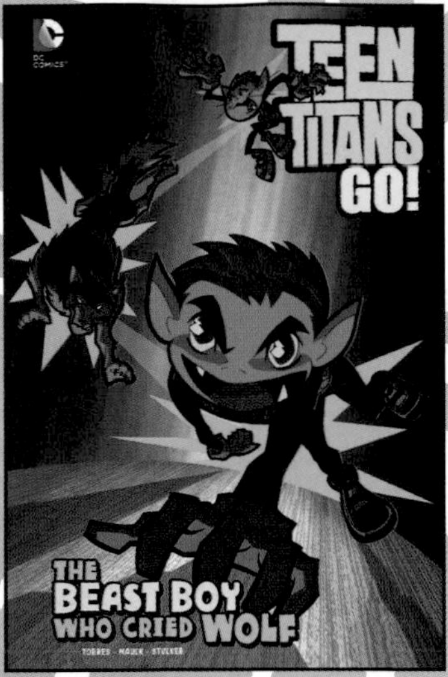
TEEN TITANS GO!
THE BEAST BOY WHO CRIED WOLF
TORRES · MAUCK · STUCKER

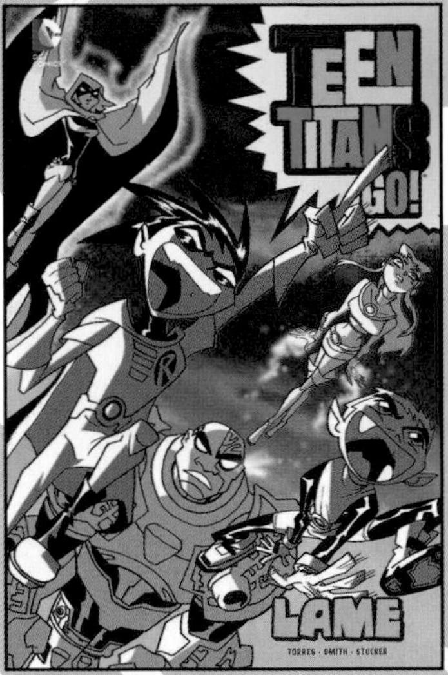
TEEN TITANS GO!
LAME
TORRES · SMITH · STUCKER

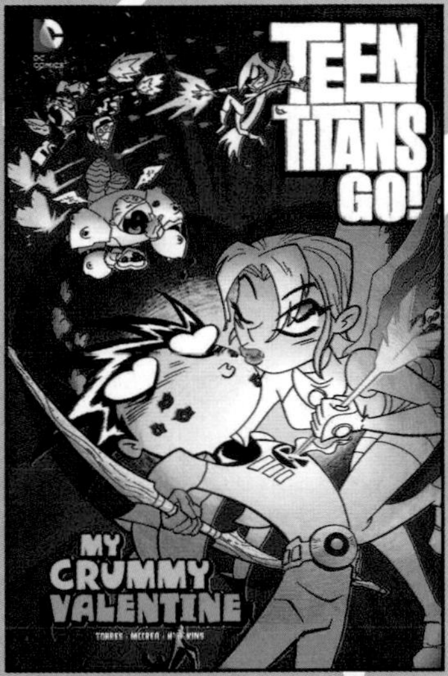
TEEN TITANS GO!
MY CRUMMY VALENTINE

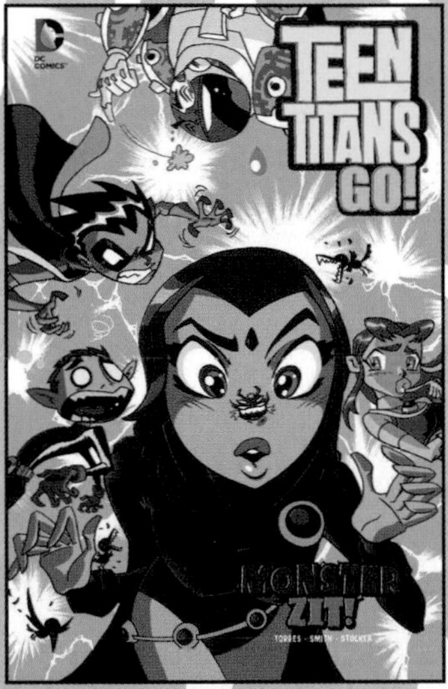
TEEN TITANS GO!
MONSTER ZIT!
TORRES · SMITH · STUCKER

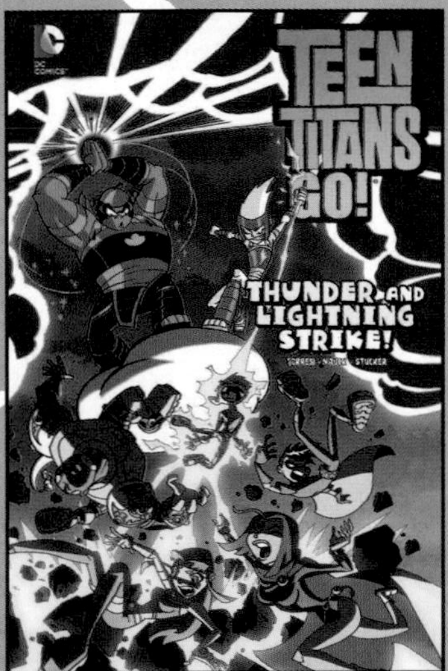
TEEN TITANS GO!
THUNDER AND LIGHTNING STRIKE!
TORRES · MAUCK · STUCKER

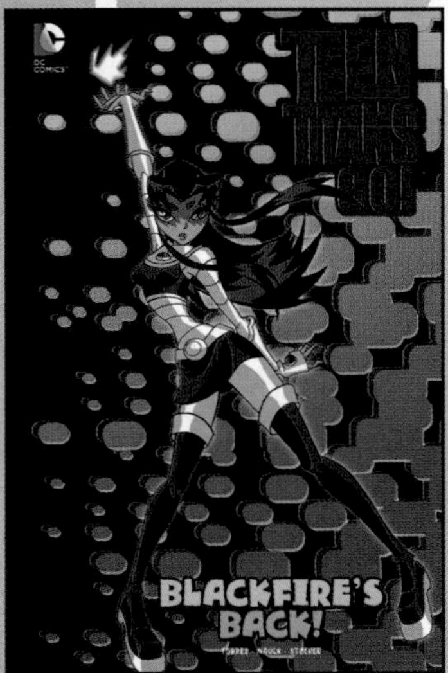
TEEN TITANS GO!
BLACKFIRE'S BACK!
TORRES · MAUCK · STUCKER

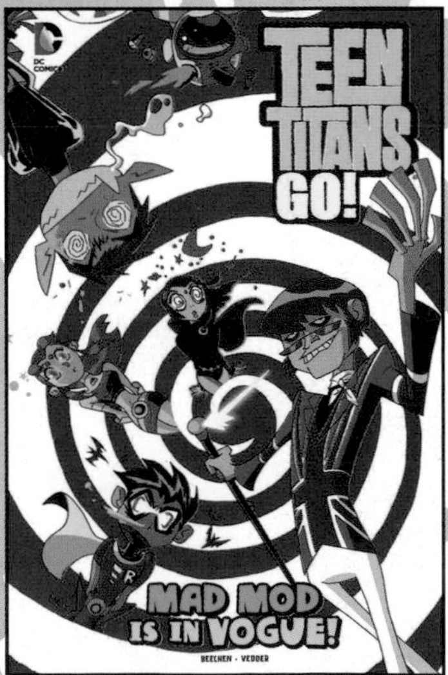
TEEN TITANS GO!
MAD MOD IS IN VOGUE!
BEECHEN · VEDDER

TEEN TITANS GO!

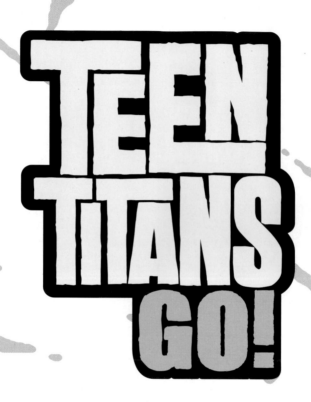